DUES

and

DON'TS

DUES
and
DON'TS

RICHARD LAUER

iUniverse, Inc.
Bloomington

Dues and Don'ts

This is a work of fiction. All of the characters, names, incidents, organizations, and dialogue in this novel are either the products of the author's imagination or are used fictitiously.

iUniverse books may be ordered through booksellers or by contacting:

iUniverse
1663 Liberty Drive
Bloomington, IN 47403
www.iuniverse.com
1-800-Authors (1-800-288-4677)

ISBN: 978-1-4620-6353-6 (sc)
ISBN: 978-1-4620-6354-3 (ebk)

Printed in the United States of America

iUniverse rev. date: 11/16/2011

Tis fate that flings the dice
And as she flings
Of kings make peasants
And of peasant kings

-John Dryden

CHAPTER ONE

Ironically, my nightmare began shortly after midnight when I was awoken from my sleep by Chief Henderson and told to get my ass down to 2 Torino Tower as quickly as possible. Why? For what? The chief never bothered to explain but as soon as I got in my car, it became all too clear without any doubts clinging to my cobwebs.

"The three Gombahs found dead in their penthouse suite," the police band screamed bloody murder. "Burned to death beyond recognition," preliminary reports vouched for three piles of dust that were once Tony Arcadio, Richie DeMasi, and Nonny Cozzi, the three richest, most powerful men in the world.

When I arrived at their World Headquarters suite, the three piles were still smoldering with a delicate trace of some sort of accelerant cleaving to the air. I cursorily presumed it a leftover remnant utilized by the killer. Upon further investigation, no bottles, cans, or any other fluid-like containers were found in the penthouse. What's more is that there were no lighters, matches, flares, or any other incendiary devices discovered that could start a fire either. Except for those three piles of dust on the boardroom floor, nothing was out of place. This was substantiated by Lilith Salome, Executive Secretary to Mr. DeMasi. She, along with Building Security, was the first on the scene. Miss Salome was also the one who originally placed the 911 call that night.

Remarkably, the fire from this portable inferno was as selective as it was reserved, for nothing in the immediate vicinity of the three piles was burnt, let alone singed. Frank Sampson, the attending coroner that night, stated that the three Gombahs' bodies reached core temperatures of 3000°C. What's equally fascinating is that not one single rumor of fire was insinuated, let alone distinguished, by any of the seven hundred smoke detectors systematically positioned throughout the penthouse. Ambrose Fossbinder, Building Engineer for 2 Torino Tower, stated the smoke alarms were so acutely calibrated that a match lit three hundred feet away could be detected—they were that sensitive. Fossbinder further related that the units were tested every hour on the hour, but as to how or why the systems all malfunctioned at once, he couldn't readily explain, not even with a Harvard-educated guess.

A slight haze continued to hector sprinkler units that, for some inexplicable reason, were also never activated. I should point out that these sprinkler units were nothing more than elaborate fire hydrants descending as stalactites from a high arched ceiling that supported a thirty foot deep retention pond on the roof. The penthouse, in many respects, resembled a bunker. Not only was it steel reinforced, it was also fireproof and bombproof. Despite taking up the entire two-hundredth floor, there was only one way in and one way out and that was through a massive six-foot thick vault door. Addison Lipscomb, Structural Engineer for Torino Tower, stated a 747 couldn't breach the Tower's defenses. I had heard of safety precautions before, but quite frankly, this bordered the paranoid. I concluded it a knee-jerk response to Osama bin Laden and September 11th. It was a logical assumption to make. After all, Torino Tower was built on the site of the old World Trade Centers.

The three Gombahs fought for every dollar, every inch, and every buyer, yet there were no scuff marks anywhere on the floor to indicate a struggle for life had ensued here less than an hour before. There wasn't even a drop of blood in the penthouse. There were also no signs of forced entry. This was indeed baffling—not only as to how the killer got in, but how he got out when the vault was secured from the inside. I couldn't reconcile a fire that burned so intensely, yet so cautiously. It was the craziest thing. It was as if the fire knew where it was going and why. I'd never seen anything like it. Fire Commissioner Patrick stated that in his thirty years investigating and fighting fires, he had never encountered such an encryptic and controlled burn. Everyone in the penthouse that night was at a loss for words to explain this madness that made no sense on any level, including and especially the two-hundredth floor.

In a traditional homicide, the body leaves telltale signs, surrendering clues like a pigeon in Texas hold 'em. In this particular case, there were no bodies, defense wounds, or physical evidence to establish a timeline of parting this world to the next. How could such things be possible in this most modern of worlds? Didn't we, after all, know everything, not only about reasons for life, but causes of death? But even without typical earmarks, I too assumed their deaths to be the result of foul play. When you did the math, it was really a no brainier. The Gombahs had it all twenty four-seven, three hundred sixty-five days a year. And wasn't that, at the end of the rainbow, the ultimate combination to success? They literally had it all: fame, fortune, power, toys, and a revolving door of the finest trophy wives money could not only buy, but keep. That alone was sufficient enough reason for me to believe their deaths were homicides. I mean, you don't just throw everything away when you've got everything to lose. It wasn't just crazy, it was nuts to think, let alone do.

Until that night, I had never met my boyhood idols. Oh sure, over the years I had seen them around town, but never up close and in person. In my wildest dreams, I never could have envisioned our initial meeting to be conducted under these bizarre circumstances. Who could have, besides God, and maybe perhaps Nostradamus?

I wanted to say a lot of things to them in my world of murderers, maniacs, and strange things that go bump in the night. But all I could muster was, "I'm terribly sorry." Nobody, especially my boyhood idols, deserved this period at the end of their earthly sentence, regardless how witchy, bitchy, or Jewish. Now, by the cruelest of twists, their deaths revolved around me. But that orbit was far from complete, no matter how many times it spun around in my head.

Despite seeing them in this mortally reduced state, I still couldn't believe they were dead. The Gombahs were not only larger than life; they were the very epitome of life. They had an incredible run of fifty years to prove it, too. Many a man would be willing to settle for king of the castle one day. Now just imagine fifty years of the finest things the world had to offer for your convenience and pleasure. How could all that be gone? How do you resolve the issue of the most influential and recognizable men in the world being reduced to dust at your feet? Needless to say, it was hard to swallow and digest. I just couldn't break them down as simple carbohydrates; they were much too complex for such naïve panderings that characterized good guys and bad guys with white and black chapeaus.

As I stood, towering over them, I just couldn't help but think how far they had come from their Spartan origins in the Bronx. If there was ever a rag to riches story, theirs' was the model and template. But even that now seemed like a million years ago when the Gombahs cut a different kind of deal and headline in the *New York Times*.

Sure, their cause of death was nebulous and murky, but their storied lives were tirelessly highlighted and chronicled. They had perpetuated a paper trail that would've envied Nazis. The Gombahs were known on every continent by people who had a more conventional fire insurance policy. In that respect, their lives held no doubt, no mystery, no suspense—their public lives that is. We all knew them like a best seller. And every year, an updated version came out to revise and tweak the old one with a New Age twist of how the three Gombahs could screw people with their pants still on.

We all knew how they originally amassed their fortunes. As a matter of fact, they perished on the fiftieth anniversary of their winning the tri-state lottery jackpot. It was said from the moment a man got out of bed, he saw, heard, tasted, or touched something the Gombahs sold, financed, manufactured, or delivered to his front door. They were the magnets to which all other precious metals were intimately attracted. We all inevitably became dervishes[1] swirling around their Svengoulian[2] glow on *Page Six*[3].

Fitzhugh Strong, Financial Analyst for the *Wall Street Journal*, claimed that when the Gombahs sneezed, Atlas got sick. They were the elephant in every boardroom, whether they were physically present or not. They were that big, that scary. There was no avoiding them, regardless of where you buried your head and toes in the sand.

In addition to being New York's favorite sons, they were the world's first trillionaires. This, by the way, was accomplished before they were thirty years old. At the time of their deaths, they had principle and controlling interests in nearly half the Fortune 500 corporations on the Stock Exchange. Their long fingers were on the pulse of every foreign and domestic market day and night. Nothing escaped their tractor beams, and if by chance anything did, it only meant it no longer registered with those one-eyed monsters lurking behind another kind of metal grate like some vigilant dragon presiding over the family jewels.

The Gombahs' penthouse was indeed worlds away from pitching pennies and shagging prodigal crumbs that missed their greasy mouths the first time around. In the Bronx in those days, there were no nigger loving liberals embracing Adlai Stevenson. There was also no mercy for mama's boys who weren't willing to beat the shit out of a Brooklyn Dodger fan for Mickey, Yogi, and Whitey[4].

From the very beginning, their lives were entangled by an invisible umbilical cord that bound them forever together. They were that close, that inseparable, grade school, reform school, and the Jersey docks. They shared the same desires, the same interests, the same birthday—they even banged the same dago broads who knew the geographical significance between Capistrano[5] and Niagara Falls.

After dropping out of high school, they slaved on the docks for seven years, looking for a remedy to being broke every Monday morning. Having nothing but bare essentials to tide you over between bread relays does tend to give a man a fatalistic approach that owns nothing outright except a pestering bark and nagging growl. Undeterred, the Gombahs sought every fix and magic bullet to cure them of their cyclical poverty. And by chance, it was a lucky shot—a one in a four-hundred-and-eighty-million lucky shot. Suddenly, just like that, three wops from Hell's Kitchen became the biggest lottery winners in history, collecting after taxes, $666 million and change. The three Gombahs then legally consolidated and joined forces under the Torino Trademark. And the rest, as they say, is history—not just any history, but our history.

How the Gombahs ever came to be the chosen ones to spread the Western word of General Motors and Coca-Cola seems like such an improbable scenario and series of events. I suppose it's no more preposterous than the Amazing' Mets[6]. Their corporate rise to power was that meteoric. Overnight, they had become a formidable three-headed monster to be reckoned with. They had become "it" in every game of corporate tag. How accomplished they had become in breaking down economic systems and showing within a fraction of a cent how much was windfall profit and how much was capital gains tax. It was uncanny how quickly the Gombahs mastered Keynesian supply-side economics. It baffled MBAs as well as business scholars. Their "take no prisoners" approach became the preamble to their bestselling book, *The Capitalist Creed*. Many were the CEOs from Enron to Halliburton who filed their fangs and tax returns on those greed breed passages of never, ever selling your self short again.

Roosevelt Dobson, Professor of Economics at Syracuse University, stated "The three Gombahs could show investors not only where the smart money was going, but where it was going to stop along the way." He further stated, "They could track a bull from Pamplona to Wall Street blindfolded." He went on to say "The three Gombahs were not only a step ahead of everyone else, but the very game itself."

The Gombahs ushered in the Golden Age of Corruption when corporate raiders could lie, cheat, steal, and kill without being held accountable legally, morally, criminally, and most importantly, financially. It was almost as if putting their tobacco-stained hands on the Bible didn't mean a goddamn thing! To their credit, they wanted to make a name for themselves, other than the one that spawned them as bastard sons who knew their whorish mothers, but never their collective father.

How could you blame them? They grew up where necessity was the mother fucker of all inventive alibis to the cops. Yet when all was said and done, they only sought what everyone else wanted: money, lots and lots of money. Seriously, who didn't want to be like those high class call girls on Fifth Avenue who blew thousands on odds and ends that would forever collect more dust than compliments?

No one really cared about means, methods, or even global warming. We were more concerned about what not to eat than who was eating the Big Apple. Forgetting what transpired before we took center stage is nothing new. The Present does have a tendency of bankrupting perspective not to mention the wheels that turned before we reinvented them.

The Gombahs essentially became our ambassadors and fearless leaders. Their graven images on poker chips at their Sin City casinos inspired even fez heads[7] from Peoria, reminding them that the whole idea behind gambling was to steal a few pots from the house, not a couple of monogrammed towels and ashtrays. The Gombahs were the very embodiment of risking everything when you had nothing left to lose. That was part and parcel of their mystique, their attraction. It also didn't hurt being tall—very tall—dark, and handsome.

The Gombahs had the world not only in the palm of their hands, but by the short hairs. How's that for a power trip? To have the ability to wipe out entire cities and towns without a bomb dropped or a single shot fired in malice. Still, we sat idly in front of our television sets as they gobbled up Corporations that had earlier devoured mom and pop stores in those Darwinian backwaters. But we liked it that way. We liked to know what we should say and when we should say it. We also liked to know what we should eat and when we should eat it with a glass of Zinfandel. Basically, it provided security and a semblance of order throughout the ranks of the soldiers of fortune. Eventually, it got to the point where we didn't even care about defining pornography whether we saw the dog and pony show or not.

The Gombahs had become powerbrokers of that first order and magnitude that could make both dreams and nightmares come true. Yet for all their wealth, they never donated money to any religious charity or civic organization. Being filthy rich, they were granted these eccentricities. Sure they were irreverent sons of bitches, but they were our irreverent sons of bitches! We just assumed they were hardworking men who said what's mine is mine—end of discussion. In a nutshell, they were tight-fisted tough guys who'd give a Bowery bum a kick in the ass before bestowing upon him their two cents. That was the extent of their charity and good will toward men.

This Torino juggernaut was not only committed, it was ruthlessly committed. Who could forget when they bought Rockefeller Plaza and had the big Christmas tree removed during the holiday season?

They desecrated and razed other city landmarks too. But really, how many times did we have to be reminded about Arab dogs, death tolls, and grieving spouses who cashed in on that ultimate death benefit that kept on giving long after guilt and culpability?

Bennett Woodcock, Math Wizard Extraordinaire at Princeton, stated "The three Gombahs made more money when they were asleep than half the world's population did while awake." During their trail blazing days, I was little more than a scalped ten-year-old kid at Saint Daniel's school in the Bronx. It was at that time that my feelings were being molded and shaped by my boyhood idols that once lived right down the street from my parents' house on Asylum and 161st.

I know it sounds jaded and no different from the six o'clock news with its choral chants of the toast of the town getting toasted. No one, though, should ever have to investigate the death of his childhood heroes. I couldn't help it. You might say I had no choice in the matter. I was cherry picked by Mayor Yates himself. And you know what they say about fighting City Hall.

Upon my arrival at Torino Tower, this story already had legs halfway around the world. Not even in death did the Gombahs go quietly into the night. This wasn't just a celebrated case, but one that was already being called the Crime of the Century.

How though you ask, is it possible to have a murder investigation without a body, or in this particular case, three? Still, the penthouse was cordoned off and ruled a New York City crime scene with prejudicial and extenuating circumstances. Never have I had so many questions badgering me at once since the Quinn sisters' murders in 1998. One local columnist insisted the Gombahs had a little too much money to burn. The speculation gamut ran from the terrorist ghost of Mohammed Atta to a deranged pyromaniac on the loose in Lower Manhattan. There were dozens of cock-eyed conjectures in the mainstream as well as on the periphery and lunatic fringe.

That's to be expected, regardless of who or what you believe deep down inside. Horseshit, after all, never changes. All that changes are the assholes who step in it.

After the meager crime scene was canvassed, processed, and eyewitness statements collected, I still didn't know what angle to pursue or who, for that matter, to play twenty questions with first. Over the years, I found twenty questions to be the tipping point in any interrogation. Sure, I encountered some tough street crews that made mimes seem like Chatty Cathy by compare. But even the tightest lipped mobsters eventually got around to plea bargaining and dropping dimes. You might say it was a rite of passage to witness relocation programs in the middle of the desert and the bottom of the Hudson River.

Had the Gombahs recently changed their wills? Were there any jealous lovers, or bitter ex-wives? Did they have any power hungry kids? What about disgruntled ex-employees? I didn't even want to think about their business competitors who wanted them permanently removed from the playing board. I didn't know where to start piecing together the events leading to the penthouse. I was working with a lot of nothing in hopes of stumbling over something besides an Evidence Response Technician. But what exactly was I looking for-a reason, a motive, or simply a logical explanation? It was too much to ask for a credible eyewitness who didn't have a drinking problem. Such pipe dreams only exist in the ideal world.

To top it all off, there were no surveillance videos of the Gombahs after they entered the lobby that night. John Ferguson, Chief of Security, stated all security cameras were knocked offline at exactly 11:57 p.m., the very moment the Gombahs entered Torino Tower. How could something already strange get stranger? How could all those state-of-the-art safety systems go haywire at the same time, and for precisely three minutes? It was as if the building was establishing its own alibi and timeline.

The next morning, this case would get even more implausible and off-the-wall. James McKay, Chief of Forensics at New York City Crime Lab, stated that a strand of black hair found in the vicinity of the three piles of dust had no known match in the genome model. McKay further related the hair sample came from something zoetic[8] and that it was most definitely carbon based.

Chapter Two

If a city never sleeps, neither does its resident evil. Welcome to the Big Apple, where insomnia and midnight oil conspire to bring about the same results with two very fundamentally opposed views on the subject. In New York, there's a reason for every indulgence and ten more to justify why a particular one was the right one at last call for alcohol.

The dance card was never blank, even when the Big Bad Bear[9] terrorized those fat little piggies on Wall Street. Every day was a Bacchanalia[10], a non-stop conveyor belt of Warholian celebrity that constantly reminded us how fleeing fame, fortune, and those jigs from Kenya[11] really were in the long run. It was said if you couldn't find it in New York, that it hadn't yet been invented. The Big Apple was the only world class city in a class by itself that forever tempted people to come take a bite, if they so dare. On and on, one world after another was assembled in New York: the Music World, the Publishing World, the Advertising World, the Financial World, the Entertainment World, the Baseball World, even the United Nations. It was as if all the cardinal points on the compass converged there as intersecting lines on a pentagram.

Why does the City come to life after the sun goes down? How did diurnal creatures ever come to rule the night? Man is indeed the unconventional animal in pursuit of a convention. Maybe darkness is to transform us back in time when clubs were not synonymous with swanky water holes and skinny ass bitches clutching cosmopolitans.

We all became ravenous after sunset, tracking our quarry and stalking our pieces of ass. Although night provided light, it was an artificial substitute, even when crocodiles were real and goodbyes sincere. New York is no place for sentimentalists. It's a tough town that doesn't tolerate mediocrity any more than happy losers who kiss their sisters and call it a moral victory. If you weren't ready the moment that curtain went up, you'd be run out of town to find a wide-hipped breeder who could cook and clean without hinting about glass ceilings or slave revolts on the horizon.

Don't get me wrong, this is not an indictment on New York, but rather a celebration of its endless diversity of possibilities. Still, someone had to draw that line between viper dens and tourist traps. Truth, wherever it's found, however, always plays to the smallest audience. Even our quest for longevity underscores the belief that only the good die young. Corruption, as I'm sure you know, only begins with the age of consent, of being old enough to bleed and old enough to butcher.

I learned as a rookie working vice in Lower Manhattan that regardless how wanton and depraved a man's desires, he could have them fulfilled for a price. As any neophyte to the streets, I was a cherry. At twenty-three years old, I was no exception. Only in New York, that learning curve was greatly accelerated. In those first months, I saw things I never saw before, not even in snuff films in the Village. And I recall thinking I knew the depths of man's erogenous zones. The perverts and degenerates in my new world were twisted like Coney Island pretzels. How warped was the reality that lied between innocence and experience?

The more money people had, the more debased their bedroom preferences. Who would've ever thought wealthy men with golden parachutes enjoyed golden showers? In the beginning, I assumed they were just trying to stay in character, albeit with the streams reversed. Maybe they had to stay golden to keep that illusion of Midas alive. Who knows? They never confided and I never bothered to ask. You might say it was a golden opportunity lost.

I suppose I didn't want to know that the good guys were as sleazy and bent as the bad ones, that girls of sugar and spice and everything nice had become bitter, languid whores of silicone, collagen, and Botox. In a sense it's true. There's no reason to gift wrap pearl necklaces when they're a surprise to both the giver and receiver. Over time, I came to the realization that we were all a little nuts and off center, but only a select group of these crazy mother fuckers had certificates to actually prove it. This perverse transparency eluded me until I stopped passing blame onto Society's ills. Then, and only then, did I become a buck richer. By then I was finished with vice and had become a homicide investigator out of Brooklyn. I know, of all the damn places! My father's still probably rolling around in his grave, having been born in the shadows of the House that Ruth built[12].

I could care less what horny fools were doing with their clothes off, as long as the participants were of legal age. I could give two shits about who was getting poked in the shorts or who liked sticking their dick in a glory hole in some seedy Greenwich dive. It only made it more interesting when it was somebody famous who regularly preached family values from the back of a high horse. People are in general more self-righteous with their pants still on. But even hypocrites on bully pulpits had needs that had to be addressed before that last precious grain of sand plummeted as some love struck lemming into the abyss of the overturned hourglass.

In Lower Manhattan, you could alter the mood to suit the occasion, like when dirty politicians said one thing off the record and another before a Senate grand jury looking into organized crime in the Garment District. Changing perceptions never allowed me the luxury to forget whose ass I had to kiss to get into Studio 54. There was no illusion about that at soirees or at swinging singles parties where clothing and Viagra were never optional. What my marks witnessed is what I projected myself to be at that particular moment in time. My show was really no different from those at Madison Square Garden. The only thing, the finished product wasn't always shiny and brand-spanking new. Just as with me, people didn't know how it transpired or originally came about. All they knew is where the gas went and where the oil came from. Beyond that tightly knit showroom circle, buyers and dealers were perplexed as to how New Age wizards were able to transform pig iron into sleek, streamlined Cougars, Mustangs, and Jaguars.

I first learned to be a changeling in vice. It was a survival technique as much as a job requirement. How else do you think cash cows and golden calves survived without being sacrificed for the common good in the Sinai? While working undercover, I had to know not only how to score, but how to keep score. They never ask how you fought, or even what you were fighting for. All they ask is, "Did you win? Did you get your man?" Style, as you very well know, only garners pity points and consolation prizes on cigarette littered shoulders.

Seriously, can there be ambushes when you already know what you're getting yourself into? Still, there's no reason for pretenses in dark alleys. When all is said and done, nobody wants to be infected with doubt any more than communist blasphemies, of nothing being something that can only be found on some snowy Tibetan mountaintop. I can still hear that Madison Avenue jingle rummaging in my head: "Do you want to be the Captain of your destiny or the second mate on the ship of fools?" We all sought instant gratification and Epicurean[13] practices that could be made perfect. Besides, there was no time to waste on untested systems and get rich schemes that dabbled in oxidized pick axes and wrinkled, old treasure maps. We were all guilty of this overdraft of excessiveness, of wanting chocolate fixes and six pack abs. Who amongst us didn't want heaven on earth right now and without priestly shoestring budgets preaching self-restraint as if it were a realistic option to contemplate?

In a way, it was reassuring to know Almighty Buck was many names, but always one familiar image that couldn't be denied or called into monotheistic question. What's more, there was never any eternal confusion in regards to paternity, virgin births, or friendly ghosts besides Casper[14]. However, there was another catch to function following form, one less profound and mystical. Seeing is believing, and there could be no claim jumpers or imposters to its worldly, regal throne. It was indeed crazy, as if we all just suddenly hailed from Missouri. If you couldn't find it, finger it, fuck it, and forget it, it served no higher purpose at company picnics or on corporate ladders.

The main drawback with that mantra is that people were always considered ballast. How is it possible to get intimate when everyone is deemed expendable? We didn't give a damn if they had a lot of baggage or just a Gucci overnighter with a vibrator and tube of K-Y jelly. But just as shiny lures are detrimental to big mouth bass, they are equally fatal to egomaniacs looking to ride into glory in the Crimean[15].

Seeing isn't exclusively reserved for the eyes. Time and distance also provide perspective, and although it may not be as physically gratifying, it nonetheless allows a man a glimpse into those worlds beyond the flesh of the street peddler. We all, though, were under the narcissistic impression that we were the masters of our Johnsons, when in fact we were nothing more than unionized shills standing vigil outside civic brothels where wage slaves were sold to the highest bidder. What we failed to realize about "residency requirements" was that bottom lines only fed another class of well-dressed predators. You have to remember, there was a dumbing down policy in effect in those days. Oddly enough, it also revolved around a Peter, a very common, if not troubling, theme.

How far had we fallen into the breach? Men and women alike were bleaching their tresses blonde as a kind of badge of honor. It became a beaded stigma befitting Nero and Caligula. Only in their sexually charged, morally bankrupt day and age, they appointed horses to the Senate, not horses' asses. We could finally say with conviction that dumbdom had a king and court complete with jokers, jesters, and dirty, old men in silk pajamas who put their own baited spin on those tumultuous waters in Hell Gate[16] that to this day still swirl as Charybdis[17] between Manhattan and Queens.

It still begged the question: had we been blindsided by sex and greed, or were we just willing to ignore the warning signs and sport designer blinders?

Did we feign illiteracy in regards to that lex scripta[18] and graffiti upon those walls beyond Babylon[19]? Perhaps we didn't want to recognize a Chair[20] that had no straps, electrical circuits, or wet sponges? Maybe we didn't want to acknowledge those religious zealots amongst us who kept insisting something was rotten before those allotted three days were up?

In short order we went from the driver's seat to being sex addicts who kept pumping out more Casanovas destined for the back one. It was such a gradual transmigration that we didn't even know we were being cooked with the holiday goose until the fork was plunged into us. "But if it feels good, it must be good for you." That, if you don't know, is the opening line of *The Capitalist Creed*. This, more or less, became our new good book to quote scripture and passages to justify our theft of Peter to pay off bookies, loan sharks, and drug dealers, other than Saint Paul.

What man doesn't long for yesterday, when pussies, not situations were tight? When hot, sticky summers were eternal, and not those tedious novels by Melville? Is it possible to recapture days lost to forever after? Still, a fool can believe in Santa Claus, the Easter Bunny, and a blue-eyed Jesus. But as the child grows out of those shoes of the fisherman, so must an old man abandon his desires of grabbing youth for all the wrong reasons.

It's said the art of seduction, like the art of conversation, is knowing when to seal the deal and spring the trap. But how is it possible to have copycats with original sin? It does smatter of contradiction as innocent pursuits at four in the morning.

For years, I too was caught between Sunday tribute and highway robbery. Whether I lost my faith, or simply misplaced it, I still don't know with any degree of certainty. I was not alone in questioning the existence of God. At the time, it was really hard to believe in anything you couldn't see, touch, or take for a test drive.

How was it possible to contemplate the meaning of life without wondering about the veracity of religion? Was the Holy Bible literal, figurative, or just another fish story made up by a dozen Jewish fisherman? But could a hoax be perpetuated for over two-thousand years with only three men being the wiser? Pulling the wool over the eyes of sheep isn't actually a talent as much as a bellwether's[21] cruel trick. But if life is the journey, then death must be its logical conclusion. Yet destiny that makes seatbelts obsolete also dismisses cautionary warnings as old wives tales.

I was far from select in this tug-of-war. Sure, my methods may not have always been admirable, but when you're rolling around in the mud with low-lifes, you have to play dirty. Please don't pigeonhole me. I believed in Miranda and the Bill of Rights, I just didn't believe they were carved in stone and brought down from the Mount by Officer Friendly.

It's true, you don't make mistakes; mistakes make you. Such admissions might sound philosophically far-fetched, but it's no more absurd than believing in level playing fields never found on any map of Rand McNally. We might very well be social animals, but we still harbor dirty little secrets destined for distant, remote shores. This is what gives voice to every damnation and Hamleted soliloquy from which all counts begin their bloodline and descent into Infinity.

CHAPTER THREE

It's not like I didn't know where I had to go. It was inevitable, as if it too was written in the stars alongside Aldebaran and Betelguese. I had come full circle, only now I was the whore in the whorehouse. The best part was I could be John Cassandra every moment of every day. I didn't have to worry about some junkie blowing my cover anymore. You don't know what a relief it is to be yourself. I also didn't have to befriend people only to betray them in court later on. Some offenders I genuinely had an affinity for, and under different circumstances it might have been the basis for a mutual relationship. It's tough to say though, because they were being real and upfront with me while I was pretending to be somebody I could never hope to be.

The difference between working vice and homicide was like day and night, like old money and nouveau riche. Sure, they might constitute the same base color, but there were a lot of shadings between those two money trees. Vice was about replaceable parts in the oldest profession in the world, whereas homicide tilted forward finality and closing the Doomsday Book on another bloody chapter that always had the same author.

Going back to where my career began dredged up a person who no longer existed except on celluloid. Still, I could find no pride in deception, even when I was in the lawful right. I could not be proud of a conviction record where deceit trumped knowledge and a man's ability to think on his feet outside massage parlors.

Being in that sordid haystack again, looking for a shiny prick didn't breed familiarity as much as it did contempt. Despite knowing where I had to go, I still didn't know who to play twenty questions with first. Should I begin at Torino Tower or *LaScalda*, that expensive Italian joint on the Lower East side that's reputedly built where Peter Minuit[22] bought Manhattan from an Algonquin medicine man for sixty guilders in 1626? Should I backtrack or should I follow in the Gombahs' footsteps? Should I begin where they were last seen or where they were first spotted that night?

Twenty-seven people saw the Gombahs between *LaScalda* and Torino Tower, and they all pretty much stated the same thing on their preliminary statements. Archibald Leach of the auction house Lord, Harry, and Gooseberry, the three Gombahs' dining companion that night, was the lone dissenter to the events leading up to the penthouse. Did he, perchance, see something the others didn't, or did he miss something the others witnessed? But as in any investigation, only time would tell who was lying and who was telling the truth.

I was never stumped right out of the gate in an investigation before, especially one of this high profile caliber. That in and of itself was cause for alarm, because everyone was watching me and waiting for results. Not even a polar bear could hunt, let alone scavenge, under these cold and frigid conditions. I never had such an abridged timeline to work with either. It was in that three minute hectic window that I had to find a killer, a motive, and a murder weapon. This, of course, was based on the premise that the Gombahs' deaths were homicides. Before proceeding with any follow up interviews, I knew I needed a prudent explanation to the cause of death that I could work with and hopefully build a case upon. Basically, I was looking for someone to rationalize this holocaust that reduced the Gombahs to cinder in a moment's flash.

Was it possible there was a third rail to explore beyond murder and suicide? To tell you the truth, I was willing to listen to anyone in order to kick start this investigation. I didn't care if it was sibyls, psychics, gypsies, or even tarot card readers from Harlem. I was desperate. But where does one go in search of the unknown and mysterious? I could only really think of two off hand, and those two paths parted company long before Galileo was placed under house arrest by Pope Urban VIII. Whereas science and religion deviated on creation, abortion, and Man's place in the Universe, they did share a common thread in this web of deceit that stretched from the Old World to the New.

Professor Otto Wilhelm of Fermi Lab advanced one theory of self-ignition, while Father Mike of St. Daniel's Parish brought forth another paradigm of fire and brimstone. There might not have been a consensus on the fire's origins, but both men readily agreed that an unusual, out-of-this-world phenomena had taken place at Torino Tower that defied both science and everything Smokey the Bear preached during his inspection tours of Yellowstone Park.

Besides the Catholic's obvious candidate and go to guy in a pinch, there was something called 'spontaneous human combustion.' I had never heard the phrase or event before, not many lay people had. Sure, I had heard of spontaneous combustion, but by adding human to the volatile mix, you got a whole other animal and meaning that could not be reproduced even with controversial wick theories[23] that substituted dead hogs for fat cats.

Professor Wilhelm stated there was no recognized categorical model to rudimentarily explain this fiery anomaly. The good professor stated that spontaneous human combustion was an enigma, a paradox that, unless physically observed in real time, would forever remain a scientific mystery right alongside dark matter, black holes and quarks. Despite being a world renowned Nobel Prize winning scientist in the advanced Field of Kinetics, Professor Wilhelm could not offer a valid explanation to the fire's origins, dynamics, or its limited yet devastating intensity that night at Torino Tower.

Speculations from fission to fusion advanced by non-funded mavericks and PhD candidates he would not promote, condone, or otherwise accept other than to briefly mention them as hypothetical possibilities that had been marginally advanced in the scientific community with little or no clinical credibility. Professor Wilhelm added that it was theoretically possible for a limited chain reaction to occur within the human body, "like a hydrogen bomb," he qualified. But only under the most ideal and proper conditions could such a cellular action occur and take place to produce this heightened molecular activity.

Although the event of spontaneous human combustion was profound, Professor Wilhelm informed me it was not atypical, that it had documented roots stretching back to Antiquity. Professor Wilhelm even downloaded several case studies of these fiery phenomena on his computer for me to review in his office. I couldn't get over the fact that a person could suddenly just burst into flames. The very thought along with those chaperoned photographs, was disturbing as all before and after shots of oxen and bouillon cubes. It was difficult accepting one being the other regardless how many times I compared side by side pictures of people and their post-mortem reduction to mole hills of dust.

Professor Wilhelm, despite being one of the smartest men in the world, was at a loss to explain how the human body consisting primarily of water could generate so much internal heat and thermal energy. Our body is generally regulated at 98.6°. If you're four to five degrees higher you're burning with a fever. Twenty-nine hundred degrees more and you're smoking like Yiddish cord at Auschwitz. How do you begin to explain that discrepancy? To what agency do you contribute that disparity from 98.6° to 3000°?

When I left the Professor's office that afternoon, the hypothetical conjectures prefaced through the astringent confines of science sounded reasonable, if not plausible. Nothing was definitive however and when eggheads in lab coats are at a loss for conclusive ten dollar words to explain something, whatever it may be, you know it's a recondite subject that only has computer models as test subjects and willing guinea pigs.

The other version espoused by Father Mike had its moments of drunken clarity too. The only difference was that he didn't have any before and after photographs documenting the horrific transformation from flesh and blood to dust and ash. All Father Mike had was faith as proxy for any physical shortcomings. The problem with that is that the Devil is the cause of everything wrong in the world. You might say it's a sure fire bet that covers all the Son of Sam[24] bases, of having no accountability for your actions and dirty deeds. How very convenient of Catholics to always have a fall guy at the ready with a rap sheet a mile long. To me, it was like crying wolf one too many times.

But where else was there to turn? I was looking for something that, as of yet, had no Greek appellation to recommend as a sickness or cure. In that regard, I could only think of Father Mike. Not only was he a pious and devout man of the cloth, he was also a scholarly Jesuit trained and seasoned in Rome where he served the Vatican for more than twenty-five years. Father Mike was equally versed in both clerical and secular matters. What's more, he was the only Catholic priest in America to have partaken in an exorcism. Father Mike successfully performed three exorcisms in Europe. However, only two were sanctioned and condoned by the Bishop of Rome, who held jurisdiction in such matters of Canon Law. Privately, the Holy Father frowned upon Father Mike for his unauthorized activity that didn't meet the Roman Catholic Church's criteria for demonic possession. However, instead of defrocking a good foot soldier, the Holy Father had Father Mike censured and exiled to St. Daniel's

Parish in the Bronx where he had been pastor since I was an altar boy in the sixth grade.

What interested me about Father Mike was he had authored several widely acclaimed books on demonic possession, satanic cults, and the black arts. So if anyone knew about strange and otherworldly things, he was definitely the man to see. To tell you the truth, Father Mike should have been teaching at Georgetown, or at least St. John's University. Being a dedicated and humble servant of the Church, he was content to combat and fight evil wherever it found him or he, it.

When I arrived at the rectory that evening, Father Mike looked troubled, if not worried about something. He informed me that he had read about the three Gombahs' deaths in the *New York Times*, yet he didn't seem the least bit phased at the intriguing possibilities surrounding their earthly departure. In a way, it was almost as if he personally knew the killer and cause of death from the beginning. Father Mike told me fire tempers a man's resolve or incriminates every last fiber and vestige of being in his eternal soul. "But as fire cleanses," he added, "it also destroys that which is the Lord's within."

When I pressed Father Mike for his take on the fiery subject at Torino Tower, he didn't hesitate or waver in his priestly conviction. He promptly asserted Lucifer was somewhere in New York City. Father Mike said he could again feel Satan's presence, but as for where, he could not pinpoint or further elaborate. He claimed he met this malevolent force three times before, but it had been many, many years, "until last night at midnight when Satan again announced himself to me."

I should point out the Gombahs' time of death was never disclosed to any media outlet. I never knew Father Mike to lie, and I had no reason to doubt his veracity now. Still, I had to clarify and make sure. Was Father Mike talking about people possessed by the devil or evil not of woman born?

"There is only one true evil," Father Mike revealed as one who has fought in the trenches on the front lines. "It's this pure evil that dilutes the weak and ambitious. Satan doesn't want followers or even disciples. Fire is Satan's only friend and ally. All Satan wants to do is kidnap another child from the arms of our Lord. Jesuits might be cunning orators, but Lucifer is fiendishly crafty and all wise in the weaknesses of man. He never rests; he is forever relentless in his pursuit of whom and what he wants. The Great Liar will say and promise you anything to steal your soul. Flattery, fame, riches, knowledge; these are just some of the sinister devices Lucifer uses to tempt man to stray from the Path of Salvation."

"You must beware my son," Father Mike forewarned, "for in your pursuit of justice, there is darkness beyond the night and where Satan is, it is not far behind."

On this ominous note, I departed the rectory, but not before Father Mike raised an interesting point of view. He told me the Gombahs weren't hiding in their penthouse, but were trying to keep someone out.—But who?—But why? Father Mike just enigmatically smiled before closing the courtyard door behind me.

Chapter Four

I may have expanded my portfolio of possible suspects and probable causes, but it still provided me with nothing concrete to build a criminal investigation upon. If anything, Professor Wilhelm and Father Mike just gave me two more bullets to play Russian roulette. I didn't know who or what to believe. Instead of things getting clearer, they got murkier and more questionable. Everything was going from the fantastic to the incredible, from spontaneous human combustion to the Devil himself. Although each man's theories and beliefs warranted further consideration, they both lacked conclusive evidence and lawful legitimacy. And with pressures already mounting from the Fifth Floor, I didn't have the time, patience, or luxury to pursue any more alternative explanations by whimsical professors or old exorcists.

What I needed was something tangible, something that could fly without wings. I required someone with legs who had no cloven hooves. I didn't necessarily have to swim in the mainstream to win any popularity contests downtown. What I needed was a warm body to follow and track, someone I could sink my teeth into without being called a vampire, or worse, a cannibal.

Since no credible explanation or physical evidence existed to confirm the cause of death, I was relegated to sifting through statements of eyewitnesses between *LaScalda* and Torino Tower. Despite a brief timeline, I had to piece together a circumstantial puzzle, which in any investigation is the hardest thing to not only create, but substantiate. Instead of doing follow-ups at the Brooklyn Headquarters, I decided to interview eyewitnesses in their comfort zones and safety nets. Over the years, I've found civilians parading through police stations to be nervous, even when they had nothing to fear or hide. The last thing I wanted was uptight people. Ideally, you want eyewitnesses relaxed and as lucid as possible, even to the point of being anally digressive. I knew I couldn't wait any longer, otherwise I ran the risk of people who already had attention spans that rivaled gnats forgetting key pieces of information.

I decided to work the timeline forward from 11:30 p.m., when the Gombahs were observed departing *LaScalda* for Torino Tower.

I began my follow-up interviews that day with Charles Pickett, the doorman at *LaScalda*. Mr. Pickett stated he never saw the Gombahs so agitated or unhappy, like they were bummed out about something, "like when a customer gets bad clams." Mr. Pickett added that the Gombahs never tipped him a plug nickel, yet that night Mr. Cozzi gave him a $1,000 tip after exiting the restaurant.

Hector Lopez, one of several valets working at *LaScalda* that night, stated the Gombahs, after a big fuss, reluctantly got into a gold stretch Bentley with a very tall guy. Mr. Lopez thought it unusual because they always left *LaScalda* in one of their own chauffer driven limousines. Two other valets, Jackie Graves and Donnell Whiteside, provided similar testimonies, only they added the driver of the gold Bentley was a "hot looking ho' with a nice set of cans."

Jesse Warrens, attendant on duty that night at Gas-and-Go, stated he overheard a heated exchange coming from the back seat of a gold Bentley while he was filling it up. Mr. Warrens stated he couldn't see through the tinted windows except for one slightly cracked in the rear. Mr. Warrens stated the Gombahs were arguing with some old dude dressed in black. The station recorded the transaction at 11:41 p.m. The charge was forwarded to the account of Mr. Archibald Leach, the owner of the gold Bentley.

Between Gas-and-Go and Torino Tower, it's generally a five minute ride. Yet, for some inexplicable reason, it took fifteen minutes to cover the same ground that night. Where else did they go? Where else did they stop? How come no one else remembers seeing a gold Bentley in the vicinity?

James Woodridge, sky cap at Torino Tower, stated that he saw the three Gombahs bolt from the back seat of a gold Bentley as if they had springs up their asses.

Cyrus Bell, head porter at Torino Tower, stated he saw the Gombahs running helter skelter in the middle of the street, without regard to their personal safety and welfare.

Ronald Hansen, Concierge at Torino Tower, stated the Gombahs darted frantically through the lobby like madmen before disappearing into their private sky elevator.

Rosa Lawns, Security Analyst for Clark Ritter, stated they fled past her like kids late for curfew, practically knocking her to the floor. Ms. Lawns added that it was as if they didn't even see her. But she wasn't sure if the Gombahs were focused, self-absorbed, or scared of something.

One eyewitness after the other basically reinforced the same thing about the Gombahs from that night. All that remained from the preliminary round up was Mr. Archibald Leach.

I'd been to auction houses before, but none as posh and ostentatious as Lord, Harry, and Gooseberry. It was Lord, Harry, and Gooseberry, and then there was everyone else. Lord, Harry, and Gooseberry wasn't just high end, it was the whole other end that people of a certain means only attained. Only the super-rich could afford such tastes never found on the regular bill of fare. Lord, Harry, and Gooseberry wasn't just exclusive, it was snooty, and for good reason. Not only was it the largest and richest auction house in the world, with satellite branches in thirty-seven countries, it was also the oldest and most prestigious, dating back to eleventh century London, where the original auction house still stands on the banks of the Thames.

Lord, Harry, and Gooseberry's claim to fame was that it had existed longer than any other institution of buying and selling things, not only in the United States, but throughout the world. It was said that no other business other than the Catholic Church had such a long and storied pedigree. Lord, Harry, and Gooseberry did in fact seem like it was here from the beginning of time or at least the conception of the United States. Over two hundred years in one location will give that everlasting impression. Being a city landmark firmly entrenched on Pearl Street, this massive edifice was steeped not only in colonial history, but a rich American tradition beginning with Mortimer Leach, who moved Lord, Harry, and Gooseberry from Philadelphia to this terminus ad quem[25] in New York City in the broiling summer of 1797.

Even in those days, movers and shakers from around the world flocked here. Even then, it was the in-place for the in-crowd. As the story went, you weren't anybody until you did business with Lord, Harry, and Gooseberry. It was more or less a prerequisite for success.

To the young and uninitiated, Lord, Harry, and Gooseberry wasn't actually a house, but rather a magnificent mansion, that over the years had grown several stories and sprouted fabulous wings. Its entire existence was dedicated to wealth and its tireless accumulation of it. The property was originally owned by the first robber baron of Wall Street, Mr. Wallace Salisbury, who also made his fortune buying and selling futures. That, however, is what made the free market system; someone had to buy and someone had to sell. It's as simple as that, even when taken to Cato Institute extremes. But, while some bid on secured margins, others stood on dangerous ledges, scanning the night skies for shooting stars to bring them salvation never found on any weekly installment plan.

When I walked through the magnificent gold doors that first afternoon, I was blinded. Lord, Harry, and Gooseberry only added to the allure of being the leading man in this ballroom dance. How could I not be star struck? From the moment I was escorted to the Main Hall, I had a classic case of what psychologists call cognitive dissonance. Everything everywhere was radiating and stunning, including the bevy of statuesque hostesses. But the truly remarkable thing is that I passed this place a million times if I passed it once, yet I never realized what existed beyond its imposing marble façade that reeked of money, of real old money.

Lord, Harry, and Gooseberry was timeless because whenever you entered it was now. Stuff, for the lack of a better word, might have been old, but it was still considered the finest in existence, like a fifteenth century samurai sword, or a seventeenth century Stradivarius violin, or a '57 Chevy in mint condition. This upscale garage sale for the decadently rich was compelling in its "you can look but don't touch" policy. I never actually thought a place could mesmerize me so. I mean, how could a city landmark so old and familiar be so intimidating and menacing?

I never beheld such drenched opulence that just so effortlessly poured off the walls. And so eclectic too! Lord, Harry, and Gooseberry was more along the lines of a museum than an auction house; at least that was my first impression. The Palace at Versailles was dulled and stunted by this endless accumulation of flushed wealth that sparkled and shined brighter than the sun. Only the Vatican had more priceless works of art by the masters of canvas. It was hard to fathom anyone anywhere surpassing this impressive collection that spanned the ages and globe. Now I understood why wealthy people flocked and migrated to Lord, Harry, and Gooseberry—this was their playground and candy store all rolled into one all-consuming offer. How much?

Lord, Harry, and Gooseberry catered exclusively to the top 1% who wanted something other than what the average man could have and hold and call his in the court of public opinion. The entire place was consecrated to the pursuit of happiness, service and lavish elegance.

"If it's good for the upper crust, it's great for the bottom line." That was the signature motto of Lord, Harry, and Gooseberry—one that was a thousand years in the making in providing the rich and famous with something that could match their standing amongst the other giants and titans of business, entertainment, and industry.

My initial encounter with Mr. Leach still clearly resonates to this day. The first time for anything tends to stick out. But anytime a hymen's ruptured, it's back dated and stored as a linchpin for future references; my inaugural meeting with Mr. Leach in the Main Hall notwithstanding.

I'll never forget when he introduced himself to me. So much jumped out and bombarded me at once, especially his size. Despite being a dapper old Englishman, he was still powerfully put together with a vise grip for a handshake. When he grabbed my outstretched hand, it was almost as if he was probing me and sounding my depths. It was the strangest sensation, like a colonoscopy, only what was crawling inside of me was very much alive. I had never met a man with such a penetrating look about him either. The flinty resolve in his bituminous eyes showed he was no more tolerant of class clowns than buyers with cold feet. Since Mr. Leach was a busy man on a tight schedule, I diplomatically apologized for the intrusion. Mr. Leach hurriedly brushed aside my apologies as an unwanted pest at a family picnic.

"Nonsense, it is I who should be apologizing for holding up the city's finest," Mr. Leach copiously countered. "Your reputation precedes you, Mr. Cassandra."

After pleasantries, apologies, and perfunctory formalities subsided, Mr. Leach volunteered his services, saying he would be more than happy to assist me in whatever way possible. The three Gombahs, or The Boys, as Mr. Leach liked to call them, were his oldest clients and dearest friends, "for fifty years," he emphatically announced.

Without additional coaxing, Mr. Leach proceeded to dutifully recount the events that night with the clarity of a creditor. He stated that when The Boys were in town, they would typically meet for a late night dinner at *LaScalda*. He noted nothing peculiar or out of the ordinary with The Boys that night. "If anything," he remarked, "it was normal to the point of being routine."

"I had my typical filet of sole in a béarnaise sauce while The Boys had prime rib, bloody and rare, the way they most enjoyed it," Mr. Leach recalled. He said they discussed their children, travel plans, and naturally, the antique trade. He informed me that The Boys were serious and avid collectors, possessing everything in size and price range from a Peruvian head hunter's shrunken skull to a complete seventy million year old Tyrannosaurus Rex.

Mr. Leach stated that The Boys always wanted to know when he was getting a new shipment. "They wanted to be the first in whatever they did, a very noble attribute, one that would make any father proud," he delightfully beamed. "After coffee and dessert, we departed *LaScalda*. Since my estate is on the way to Torino Tower, I insisted The Boys accompany me," he concluded.

When I pressed Mr. Leach about why the three Gombahs abruptly exited his vehicle in the middle of the street that night, he stated the traffic was extremely congested around Torino Tower, and

The Boys were expecting a very important conference call from the Tokyo Stock Exchange at midnight. "That," Mr. Leach explained, "is why the sevens preceded the sixes[26]."

I should note that the entire time I was interviewing Mr. Leach; he was pacing up and down the Great Hall. A caged panther would be more at ease than this proverbial tempest in a teapot. I've heard of restless leg syndrome before, but this was ridiculous. I'd never seen anything like it. Honestly, the guy never stood still, never sitting on his ass, or pausing on his laurels. He was mercurial, forever in motion like a prize fighter circling his opponent for a weakness to exploit. Mr. Leach was making me dizzy, just watching him. At the time, I summed it up to British quirks. You know, like bad food and rotten teeth.

Another thing, despite being friendly, Mr. Leach never really shed his reserved demeanor and stiff upper lip. If anything, he just relaxed his patrician pretenses, even when he wasn't sticking to the intimate details of every well-rehearsed fact. However stern in his stuffy comportment, Mr. Leach was not without his charms. He was too well bred to be a rude host to unexpected guests or unwelcome intruders. Make no mistake, though, Mr. Leach made it absolutely clear from the outset that he was in fact the alpha male. At first, I thought maybe that's why he didn't like to sit, but even then he would have been imposing. I mean for Christ's sake, the guy was over seven feet tall!

A man is known by many names, but he is also known by his scent. That first day, I recognized a familiar odor, but from where I couldn't readily place. As crazy as it sounds, the pungent bouquet permeated throughout the mansion as if it too were a living, breathing entity. It was primarily centered and pronounced upon Mr. Leach. That struck me somewhat peculiar because for one, we never met, and secondly, we didn't move in the same social circles.

What was also weird was that every room in the mansion had a huge, stone fireplace. I'd never seen such a hot commodity afforded one man before. Incredibly, the fires all seemed to burn at the same level and degree of intensity. This, I should mention, was accomplished without any visible source of wood or any other combustible material. If I didn't know any better, I'd swear those flames were a special effects parlor trick played on unsuspecting guests. Because of this luxury, everything in the mansion, especially the marble floors, were very warm to the touch. Mr. Leach explained the old mansion required continuous blasts of dry heat to burn off excess humidity in the air so precious treasures and other valuable works of art would not be damaged by mold and mildew.

The manner in which Mr. Leach decidedly spoke, along with his authoritative command of the King's English, made everything sound so formal and official. You could no more question him than doubt him. Mr. Leach was that convincing, that good. In all my years on the force, I never encountered anyone as eloquent as Mr. Leach. Not only was he physically slippery, he was mentally cagey, like when he sardonically sneered he was an active trader in livestock, "capitalist pigs to be exact."

I couldn't get over the enduring notion that Mr. Leach was just toying with me before the final spinal tap. I may have come on police business to question him, but by the end of my first visit, I was the one getting grilled about likes, dislikes, and what I wanted more than anything else in the world. Mr. Leach was first and foremost a salesman, one who could adopt a gray position between bottom lines and deadlines without actually seeming involved in the process of a fool parting ways with his money. We might have begun by discussing that night in question, but invariably we strayed, not only from the Main Hall, but from the three Gombahs. I may have gotten the conversational ball rolling, but after my opening verbal salvo, I never again controlled the conversation's tempo, direction, or topical flow. I was for all intent and purposes relegated to flotsam on the River of No Return.

You have to remember, I was a guest, so naturally I had to defer and grant Mr. Leach these indulgences even when they included yanking my chain. Besides, men who could change names into numbers so easily were to be respected. Although Mr. Leach was an old man, he was not to be taken lightly. There were certain men you just didn't screw with, regardless which side of the aisle they preferred in courtrooms. Mr. Leach was also a well-connected rich man with a gavel in his hand. This put him in that "do not disturb" category alongside diplomats, politicians, and Wasp nests[27].

Needless to say, Mr. Leach was a steadfast proponent of top notch and first class. To him, there was no other way to travel and go through life. Mr. Leach informed me, "quality isn't expensive; it's priceless." What better man to know this quintessential fact than one with a keen interest and very dry sense of humor? It was a natural progression even when it wasn't necessarily on the up and up. Still, in spite of these vexations, Mr. Leach was proud of the service he provided to the Four Hundred who spilled out of Astor's Ballroom[28]. Mr. Leach was also extremely knowledgeable, regardless the person, place, or topic. He not only knew what people of good taste needed, he knew what they wanted, and more importantly, when they wanted it most. In that sense, Mr. Leach was a very articulate man without peer, a rather remarkable achievement for a man of his advanced years.

Mr. Leach knew buyers and sellers around the world. He also knew places and dates of transactions like it was nobody's business. He put the memory of a scorned woman to shame. He wasn't just lobbing horseshoes or hand grenades either. Mr. Leach personally recounted every hand and every piece of silver in it. It was an exceptional talent that never once consulted a cheat sheet for assistance or mental refreshment.

Mr. Leach was a font of information in regards to the Gombahs too. He told me things about them I never knew, and I read their autobiographies cover to cover. From such tidbits and scraps, I thought I might possibly find a lead, or perhaps a suspect to pin another kind of tale on—one that would stick in the minds of a jury of liberal jackasses. They say, however, "When you're on a roll, to make sure it ain't a dinner roll."

Before departing, Mr. Leach told me if I had any further questions regarding the Gombahs to feel free to call on him day or night. Mr. Leach was not a suspect or person of interest at this time. If anything, I considered him an oddity, a curio, just like everything else at Lord, Harry, and Gooseberry.

How nice and tidy was my initial housewarming visit. It was, how should I say, time management with a flowchart, that after a Cook's tour[29] of the mansion, I was deposited back at the front door where I had entered some three hours before. The only thing is that this final product was flawed by design issues and a mass marketing campaign that fed regular Joes a different kind of nectar and ambrosia.

My first meeting with Mr. Leach, as those that would subsequently follow, would last anywhere between much too short and not nearly long enough. I did have some reservations concerning Mr. Leach, but it was nothing to pursue with a warrant. Nonetheless, it was worth noting for future references. But really, I couldn't see anything wrong with Cuban cigars accompanying the smell of success. A little corruption was not like being a little pregnant. Besides, greased palms made things run smoother in the give and take of life. That's another corporate constant that guides distant buyers to foreign markets where people as products are sold by the pound. But, while one rape of innocents was considered a necessary evil to make both sides meet in the middle, the other was purely pleasurable in its insatiable lust for virgins and new hunting grounds.

Chapter Five

Mr. Leach's statement of the events that took place that night explained some things, but not everything. Other eyewitnesses in and around Torino Tower stated the Gombahs were running *from* something, not *to* something. There's a big difference. Some stated a primal fear was in their eyes, while others swore an all-out panic accompanied their every rabid step. That's what I found so hard to believe. The Gombahs didn't walk fast, let alone run for anyone, especially after the ten course meal the maître d' at *LaScalda* stated they had eaten. You just don't pick up and run after inhaling a supper that's comparable to those condemned to the gallows at dawn. It had to be something more pressing and urgent than a conference call from Tokyo, but what? That bothered me to no end. I mean, you just don't risk life and limb for a stupid phone call. Besides, if it was that damn important, why did they wait until 11:30 p.m. to leave *LaScalda*? For the life of me, I couldn't let that go. Was it possible that the Gombahs lied to Mr. Leach? Or was Mr. Leach lying to me?

What also disturbed me was why Mr. Leach never made any reference to the shouting match that night in his Bentley. Perhaps it was just a friendly disagreement that got a little out of hand amongst old bulls. It's been known to happen; people holler and scream at one another, then five minutes later they're kissing and making up as if nothing ever happened to the apple cart. But why didn't Mr. Leach allude to that incident when everything else between *LaScalda* and Torino Tower was structured in lavish detail? Was he perhaps embarrassed by the incident? Or was it so innocuous that it needed no further mention? I knew it didn't escape him. He had a mind like a steel trap, and what went in stayed there. I could no more believe him forgetting that heated exchange than cows flying or the Gombahs running to catch a midnight conference call from Tokyo.

Several other things struck me as somewhat peculiar after my visit that day. It took me a good half hour to gather my faculties after I departed Lord, Harry, and Gooseberry. It was a queer sort of feeling, as if something was releasing its grip upon me. I don't know how else to explain it. The whole time I was inside, it was like I was under a kind of hypnotic spell. Not only did I lose all sense of time, I also couldn't logically function and process information in my customary manner. The moment I entered Lord, Harry, and Gooseberry, I could immediately feel something pulling on me. But it wasn't my heart strings being tugged; it went much deeper than that target of Cupid.

Another thing was the uncanny similarities between Mr. Leach and his ancestors who adorned the walls of the Main Hall. The resemblances were striking and remarkable by any standard measure of cubit[30] or Mendelian pea. I could see the physical traits of father and son successfully transferred and carried over the generational threshold. But generation after generation, hundreds of years removed defied genetic probability. All that seemingly changed was the amount of hair on their faces and heads. All else, including their dark and riveting eyes, were a continuous penetrating characteristic that bridged grandfathers to grandsons. It was as if they posed for eternity's easel without mutation or variation. It seemed as if Mr. Archibald Leach was the same subject, only in different periodic costumes and poses, even the ones commissioned by El Greco, Rembrandt, and Michelangelo.

Lord, Harry, and Gooseberry, like a time machine, took me back hundreds, if not thousands of years. I had never seen such old things before. Oddly enough, the older the piece, the more expensive it was at auction. How was it possible to live in a world of "the newer the better" only to discover a parallel world that valued and coveted the old, wrinkled, and long in tooth? It defied explanation. Not only that, it deliberately ran against the very grain of sexy, muscular consumerism. How was it possible that something you bought last year was deemed a worthless piece of shit, while something thousands of years old was considered priceless by men with deep pockets and narrow views?

I thought it was an inside joke with a punch line only rich people were privy to, like when blue chip stocks are about to tank and go belly up. What else could it be, right? What was the sense of owning something if you couldn't use it and abuse it? Consumerism is, after all, about disposable things, even when cash is king. It's about new car smells and patent leather shoes that have to be broken in. It's about love at first sight at "see level" where the only digging a man has to do is in his pocket. It's about beating odds and rented mules. It's about punching clocks, battling traffic, and pounding concrete. It's about standing vigil in the freezing rain all night long for the latest computer game that hasn't even hit the shelves. That's what the struggle and fight's all about, or at least that's what they told us it was about on their way to Switzerland.

I considered every possible reason why anyone would want to own a relic of yesterday. Was it simply beauty being subjective and limited to the eye of the beholder, or did it have something to do with man's selfishness and greed to have a cut of the spoils that no one else could lay claim? How do you justify spending one million dollars on a Honus Wagner baseball card? It's rare, but so is common sense, and nobody's breaking the bank to obtain that.

Between doubt and deduction, you could place the Rock of Ages and still have ample room for nut houses where people are prone to

Napoleon complexes that have no second mortgages. After that first round of interviews was complete, I still didn't know who or what to believe. If you're too analytical, you lose compassion; if you're too personal, you lose perspective. And, if you're too undecided, you lose your fucking mind!

Every thought I had was in a constant state of flux. I was ensnared in a perpetual transitional stage that had no second acts. If eyewitnesses hadn't observed Mr. Leach driving away in his gold Bentley that night, I no doubt would have pressed him further. I knew if I resorted to those strong arm tactics with Mr. Leach now, he would just lawyer up and take the Fifth. Due to that and other mitigating circumstances, I had to concede and pull back on the throttle. Remember, at the time I was looking for a killer, not a liar. Still, I couldn't forget that lies had a tendency of breeding like rabbits. And if that were the case, what else was Mr. Leach lying about, and why?

Over the course of the next several weeks, I canvassed Torino Tower, Lower Manhattan, and did more follow up interviews to see if someone in the interim might have remembered something in regards to that fateful night. But not only were the vast majority of statements replicated, they were repeated verbatim to show, to prove rather that nothing had been embellished with the passage of time. Only Greg Lauderdale on the janitorial staff at Torino Tower that night added to his previous statement. He vaguely remembered hearing Mr. DeMassi say they had "three fucking minutes" before he, Mr. Cozzi, and Mr. Arcadio disappeared into their private sky elevator never to be seen alive again.

I couldn't help but think those three minutes were somehow relevant and involved.—But how? That was another bitch that kept nagging and ragging on me. Was it perhaps an allusion to that conference call from Tokyo Mr. Leach mentioned? Miss Sheila Benson, Head of Communications at Torino Tower, stated no overseas calls were forwarded to the penthouse after eight o'clock that night, which coincidently was the same time the Gombahs departed for *LaScalda*. So that finally lay to rest that theory of why the Gombahs were running to the penthouse. Still the question remained: what was the significance and importance of those three minutes that spooked them and made them take notice? What were those three minutes in relation to? That was now the million dollar question.

Although one mystery was solved, I still had nothing substantial to build a case, much less a model upon. I reluctantly began leaning more and more towards spontaneous human combustion as the Gombahs' cause of death. What else did I have? I wasn't only at an investigative impasse; I was at a dead end. Despite its scientific pedigree, spontaneous human combustion was the only thing I had at this juncture that now made any sort of sense.

This road less traveled would eventually twist and turn until it brought me to New York University's Archives Department, where this strange and unusual event had more detractors than adherents. I discovered a rich vein that, like Professor Wilhelm said, "Stretched back to Antiquity." If this, by chance, was to be the ultimate contributing factor in the Gombahs' mortal demise, I wanted to do my homework. Mayor Yates was not a tolerant man who gladly suffered fools. He campaigned on a no-nonsense law and order platform. Ex-prosecutors from the DA's office were all alike. You couldn't cookie cut those jag-offs any more perfectly. So I had to make sure, damn sure, that I knew what I was talking about when I presented my findings to the Mayor and Chief.

The first recorded account of spontaneous human combustion was in England in the year 1067, when the eldest son of William the Conqueror was found burned to death at his castle in Sussex. The reasons and explanations in the early days of this fiery phenomena, I should point out, were centered exclusively on fire breathing dragons, just as those fought earlier by St. George. How reliable, though, were such narratives that bordered the sketchy and superstitious?

More to the point, could they be taken seriously in today's world filled with naysayers and debunkers? But even into the modern era, those fabled wyverns[31] and serpents were chronicled to rival candle and wick theories. Some things, as you very well know, never die, regardless of how many belts you tie around their necks or how many stakes you pound into their hearts.

I divided the two hundred and twenty-one cases in the NYU archives into two groups, Old World and New World. Some anecdotal yarns from the early days of this fiery occurrence were still applicable where not even a peep betrayed a hot foot. I began to see how ignorant people could personify this feverish antagonist. It was easy enough to do with what they had at their limited disposal. That's the remarkable thing about ignorance; it's never at a loss for words or short on explanations to the contrary. As you know, there's more than one way to go to hell; rubbing two sticks together is just the most common practice.

Until the Age of Enlightenment muddled, over indulgent tales of fire breathing dragons were standard issue from word of mouth to feathered quill. Then a new bumper crop began minting their own stories to explain away these superstitious remnants that lingered from the Dark Ages. These new-fangled conclusions also had glaring chasms and serious omissions that couldn't be bridged by post-mortem observation or hypothetical transferences. There are just some things you can't put through the rigors of a syllogism[32]. Still, scientists tried explaining the unknown with familiar catch phrases to counteract the aftershock of legends, myths, and a God of the gaps fraternity amongst self-denying scribes.

Spontaneous human combustion might have been rare, but it was only rare among princes and other nobleman, like gout and guillotines. As I pored over these Old World cases, I began to notice another pattern forming. The dates tended to follow a subscribed order like Halley's Comet and biblical locust. It was a profound sort of clockwork that had shorter intervals running among longer revolutions. Every incident in the Old World held steady in this devotion to one timely cycle or the other that lasted either twelve or twenty-five years. The years of duration pin-wheeled around each other like wanderers in the Milky Way:

1067, 1092, 1104, 1129, 1141, 1166, 1178, 1203, 1228, 1240, 1252, 1264, 1289, 1314, 1339, 1364, 1376, 1401, 1413, 1425, 1450, 1462, 1487.

It was incredible how exact and orderly was this culling of "liar, liar, pants on fire." How could such a supposedly random act be so precise and right on schedule? It was as if the flame had a date with destiny. And always, without fail, it was at the same time: midnight!

I read on into the night when another distinction began to emerge and manifest itself. A tall, dark figure was generally observed lurking in the vicinity where the torched victim was last seen alive. This shadowy apparition was always witnessed shortly before the witching hour.

Now we all know "tall" is open to suggestion. The question was, tall in relation to whom, basketball players or midget wrestlers? Regardless the back story, the same spectral image was reported across the ages. These static sightings were exclusively reserved for the Old World until 1492, when a new order and chronology began to establish itself and take timely shape in twenty-one and fifty year increments. It was as if the years in the New World were also suspended in Baltic amber:

1492, 1513, 1563, 1584, 1605, 1626, 1676, 1726, 1776, 1797, 1818, 1860, 1910, 1960.

How was it possible to compile all this rare data and not fully analyze it? Were men of science that blind in their pursuit of causes and effects to neglect all other aspects and points of view? What other reason could there possibly be for this apparent shortcoming?

The first well documented case of spontaneous human combustion in America occurred in Philadelphia on July 4, 1776, when the richest plantation owner in the rebel colonies, Cyrus Randolph Wolf, was found smoldering in a local hotel room in Penn Square. What gives this hotly debated incident credibility is that Thomas Jefferson and John Adams were the first men to discover his charred remains when he failed to appear at Independence Hall to sign the Declaration. I should note that Thomas Jefferson and John Adams died fifty years to the day of this discovery. There were earlier cases in the New World, but these accounts by conquistadors, savages, and missionaries were spurious at best. I pretty much dismissed any reports of spontaneous human combustion prior to the 1700's in colonial America, and treated them as one would a ten-year-old boy with an overly active imagination. And just as in the Old World, the only ones affected by this strange and unusual fiery event were wealthy people; talk about a pond hopping prejudice.

The cases in America from 1776 forward culminated with the fiery demise of super industrialist J.J. Frederick aboard his regal yacht, *Fat Chance*, off Martha's Vineyard in 1960, which coincidentally was the same year the Gombahs struck it rich. Now, fifty years to the day later, they're burned to death. How could something already beyond belief get even more unbelievable? As I sat there absorbing this data, I still didn't know how to interpret it. To say it surprised me was an understatement. I was totally caught unaware. How could I have been so blind? We all, though, have blind spots in our mirrors, whether side view, rear view, or vanity.

There were a host of ramifications and what-ifs to consider. In an ordinary, by-the-numbers murder investigation, I would've never given these preposterous allegations an audition, much less an audience. This case, however, was far from ordinary and run-of-the-mill. Besides, after weeks without credible leads or suspects to grill, I was just about ready to jump on any bandwagon, regardless which goddamn direction it was headed.

Of all the cases my good name and reputation hinged upon, it had to be this one. It was the worst case scenario imaginable: a rich man with powerful friends in high places. Unless you're committing career suicide, it's something that sane and rational men just don't do, not even under ideal conditions when you have motive, opportunity, fingerprints, and photographs. Yet there I was, headed rudderless into this perfect storm, risking everything on conjecture, speculation, and another kind of pig theory[33]. It just didn't seem right. It just didn't seem fair, but then again, the only thing fair in life is game.

But how could I refuse to explore the possibilities; the midnight hour, a tall, dark figure? There were just too many coincidences for my liking. Thomas Jefferson at the subsequent inquest stated, "Mr. Wolf, a good Virginian and loyal patriot, was last seen with a Big Brit at Hogshead Pub the night he was killed. Afterwards, the Big Brit was never seen again, at least not in Philadelphia. Years later, twenty-one to be exact, Lord, Harry, and Gooseberry opened their doors in New York City in 1797. The same year, Mr. Wallace Salisbury was found burned to death in his New York mansion. The timelines just kept clicking at twenty-one and fifty year intervals.

Mr. Leach was with the Gombahs just before midnight too. By his own admission, he stated he knew them for fifty years. Not fifty-one, not fifty-two, but fifty! Now those three minutes were beginning to make sense. The Gombahs weren't running to or from something. They were running for their lives. But how did they know?

Was I getting warm, desperate, or was my overpopulated imagination simply running away with me? So much was going through me like shit through a goose: the possible, the impossible, and the out of this world. But if my deductions were correct, I had no time to waste because after the barbeque, the Pyromaniac went underground to hibernate like a cicada once again.

Chapter Six

Regardless of where the clues led me, I was inevitably dragged back to Lord, Harry, and Gooseberry. In short, I had become a boomerang, back for another godforsaken toss. Needless to say, Lord, Harry, and Gooseberry soon became my sole destination and one stop shop, but always under the pretense of finding out more about the Gombahs in hopes of providing closure, a stylized word often bandied about in those days to help grieving survivors find a common grave site for their hysteria and salty pathology.

Soon, I too was a daily face in the mansion. As a matter of fact, I became such a familiar fixture that a designated chair and spot of aromatic English tea would be awaiting me. My guise was so disarming that I was able to nourish causal covenants with some of the wait staff who I got to know on a first name basis without any clumsy ceremonies. Through these casual contacts, I was able to glean things I wouldn't have otherwise been able to. Being a special guest of Mr. Leach allowed me enough wiggle room to move around the mansion without interferences from suffocating guides or other nine-to-five drones.

Mr. Leach's schedule, although crowded and conflicting, allowed me twenty to thirty minutes, sometimes an hour. Let me just say this on the subject: a measly crumb with the sagacious Mr.

Leach was food for thought, not only for the time being, but for all the time to come.

Our "fireside chats" sound so antiquated now, despite them being so very fresh in my head. Mr. Leach didn't mind these social interruptions; quite the contrary. He seemed to delight and relish the opportunity to once again talk about The Boys. How he would rant and rave and champion their earthly accomplishments, including global warming, which, during their fifty year acid reign of terror, increased fifteen degrees worldwide. Climatologists never saw such a dramatic spike in the macro climate. Heat waves not only started earlier, they lasted longer. Year after year, one infernal summer followed another into the meteorological record books. No one could recall such unrelenting, dry heat. When Mr. Leach talked about this environmental disaster and hydro-carbonated consequence, his dark embers glistened and radiated. It was as if he was being kindled by a burning passion beyond treasured antiques and Virginian auction blocks.

I never observed this side of Mr. Leach. I didn't know if it was his other side, you know, his underbelly and sentimental soft spot, or just merely another facet of his complicated and complex being he was intentionally allowing me to glimpse. With Mr. Leach, there was always a rejoinder attached to hang tags. Was the show-and-tell genuine, or was he just blowing more smoke up my ass? Don't forget, any man who's hard to corner is also hard to pin down. Mr. Leach was no exception to that Greco-Roman rule. He, however, could just as easily morph back into his prior state of red and black bottom lines. A chameleon by contrast was but a recent byproduct of this colorful development. That's how fast is that metamorphosis from Light Bearer to Dark Prince, from Son of God to son of a bitch.

During my visits, I had no choice but to follow Mr. Leach around as he tirelessly paced the mansion. Not only that, but I also had to make it seem as if I wasn't studying him. I have to confess, it was a task in itself. Not only did I have to appear friendly, but I also had to remain vigilant without being intrusive. I couldn't tip and expose my hand when I was a four flusher bluffing a full house of Kings over Queens. Let me tell you, it was very unsettling watching someone doomed to a life with no sweet dreams on Cloud Nine. That's probably why Mr. Leach was in such remarkable shape; it was a mixture of Stairmaster and Pilates all rolled into one exercise regime.

The jury was still out in regards to who I was to Mr. Leach. Was I another prop?—Another foil?—Another potential customer? Why was I being courted and groomed? I couldn't rid myself of the feeling that I was being drawn to Lord, Harry, and Gooseberry by a hidden agenda that went beyond law and order and the three Gombahs. I mention this because when the tables were turned away from The Boys, Mr. Leach became an entirely different person. The way he would gawk at me was obscene, almost lewd! He then appeared as a bloodthirsty beast that couldn't take his dilated, gluttonous eyes off me. I was looked upon as more than just a piece of meat hanging out to dry. It was morbid, as if he was sizing me up for something other than a coffin. In the Eden Room one night, Mr. Leach informed me that once a man achieved the pinnacle of success, "nothing but the very best would soothe his hungers and midnight cravings."

Our series of walk-and-talks became a crash course in the lives of the Gombahs. It also became a recruiting seminar to take another good paying customer away from a rival competitor. This tug-of-war was loopier than a dirty politician on a soapbox.

As you know, Crimes of the Century tend to take on a life of their own, for better or worse. Some days, I had to wait a couple of hours just for a meager twenty minute session with Mr. Leach. It was during these unattended lulls that I embarked on my little fact-finding missions. Unfortunately, I could only browse in areas not cordoned off by intimidating, black velvet ropes. I've often wondered what other treasures resided behind those gilded doors. Let me tell you, the proposal was very tempting, even when I was already surrounded by an Underworld Kingpin's ransom that would have shamed Donald Trump.

Unlike the other gilded doors throughout Lord, Harry, and Gooseberry, only one was labeled "Employees Only." In addition to that, it was the only door where a continuous din and putrid stench was freely emitted. Initially, I assumed the door led to the boiler room. Judging by the vibrations and smell, it seemed logical enough. How, though, could a furnace churn without smoke billowing from the chimney? It was the craziest thing. But what else was to be expected in a world of fantasy and make believe that eclipsed all rumors of reality? The truly remarkable thing about all this is that I prided myself on being good with sounds and smells, especially dirty rats, rotten eggs, and skunks. I was, after all, renowned and mentioned in the same breath as that fabled dick of Sir Arthur Conan Doyle. My most famous cases were the stuff of police academy textbooks. Some even seeped into urban legend.

Yet that pervasive odor, although familiar, was estranged, like it was trying to elude me or something. I can't prove it, but I believe its source was intentionally being dulled by some foreign agency. Unlike sound and smell, my sense of sight was never hampered, encumbered, or severed at the cellular level. If anything, it was heightened and invigorated, where every item in every parlor was visually magnified. Every gallery was stunning and sensational. Every room was scene-stealing, regardless if you were a red carpet Civic Opera Prima Donna or an off-Broadway ham.

Wherever I focused, there was eye candy. I couldn't turn or go anywhere without becoming a full-blown diabetic. It was that sweet without ever being cloying or saccharine laced. I never knew where to look first or turn next. It became a competition between my job, my God, and my darkest secrets and desires.

Paintings, busts, sculptures, and precious gems ensconced in Tiffany exhibition cases were on display in every staged room. Every work of art was refined to perfection. Bronze statues were so real and incredibly lifelike, not only in size and scale, but visage and intimate appeal. One in particular, in the Main Hall, depicted a forlorn man carrying an apple. Not surprisingly, Mr. Leach claimed this was his most prized catch. The dejected man looked as if he were captured in real time and not an artist's rendering sometime afterward.

There were treasure troves all throughout Lord, Harry, and Gooseberry, but the Main Hall was the capstone jewel in its tiara, the crowning achievement, if you will. It was also the Grand Gallery of Who's Who in History. Here, the most famous clients of Lord, Harry, and Gooseberry were showcased. But it wasn't showing off and name dropping affiliations as much as displaying souvenirs to be fawned over by a greater hunter who forever utilized the same method of operation and dispatch regardless of the two-legged game. The golden walls in the Main Hall were a roll call of A-lists down through the centuries. William the Conqueror, Queen Elizabeth, Henry VIII, Catherine the Great, Frederick the Great, Peter the Great, Lorenzo the Magnificent, Ivan the Terrible, Ferdinand and Isabella, Michelangelo, Galileo, Rembrandt, John Jacob Astor, John D. Rockefeller, Joseph P. Kennedy, Shakespeare, Stalin, Hitler, Mussolini, Dante, Milton, Napoleon, Ford, Washington, Oppenheimer, the three Gombahs.

I could fill a dozen more pages with celebrated names such as those mentioned above. I never realized the extent of Lord, Harry, and Gooseberry's clientele. It was the mother lode of famous people to ever grace the covers of *Time*, *Life*, *Vanity Fair*, and Lincoln's Bedroom. It was quite an achievement, despite the unusual circumstances surrounding their unveiling to a third party.

I had never realized the physical similarities between Mr. Leach and the three Gombahs. Not only were they all extremely tall with shocks of black hair, they also had the same distinctive penetrating eyes that had depth, but depth that was dark, very dark, like a Great White's. I couldn't believe my eyes, and I was never an atheist before. Was it possible? Could it be possible? Were they somehow related?—But how?—And through who? Some things, as some answers, were so out of my range that for all intent and purposes they could have been from another league.

As I said before, the moment I walked into Lord, Harry, and Gooseberry, I knew I was in another's element, one that couldn't be found on any Atomic Chart. It's true, the rich do indeed move in different circles from me and you. It might not be as crude or vicious, but it's lethal nonetheless. After all, Blood Diamonds, like Hope Diamonds, are created by the same internal forces of high pressure and extreme heat.

The more I explored, the more I came to the realization that Lord, Harry, and Gooseberry was nothing more than an extended trophy room. Don't get me wrong, the mansion had everything you could dream or dream possible. It gave new meaning to Heaven on Earth, and without delay or Sunday shakedown. How attractive was that proposition? All you had to do to obtain this paradise was give up something you'd always heard of but never seen. How's that for a bargaining chip? Everything you see for something you'll never have to worry about again. What desperate man wouldn't take that bait?

Really, who hasn't thought about fortunes outside of Chinese takeout? Or fame beyond a lifetime? That forbidden fruit was there all along too, only it already had a notch in it. How I never noticed it before still bewilders me. My whole career up to that point was predicated upon attention to detail. I was used to seeing things others didn't, couldn't, or refused to. When in Lord, Harry, and Gooseberry, I don't think I was ever actually firing on all six cylinders[34]. In my defense, the Bronze Man, or "Exhibit A," as Mr. Leach gleefully alluded to the solitary figure, was but one of ninety-three million exhibits on display in the mansion.

My mental faculties were further withered by those buzzing squads of tantalizing arm charms flaunting their crafts throughout the mansion. These bewitching beauties only added to Lord, Harry, and Gooseberry's diabolical allure by speaking volumes without once betraying any company secrets. Like Mr. Leach, they were clad in black, only they were outfitted in snug, leather-and-lace ensembles. Not only were these hostesses exotic and drop dead gorgeous, but they also possessed a demure sophistication that could simultaneously hold more than two opposing thoughts and drink orders. Beyond their winsome, inviting smiles and enchanting voices, they were intimidating as all man-eaters, only I'm not talking about the garden hose variety. Lilith Salome was reputed to have fractured from their twenty-four-karat ranks several decades earlier, yet when I interviewed her that night at Torino Tower; she looked no more than twenty-three years old. Talk about timeless beauty. It was as if time altogether forgot about her. Such was her eternal sex appeal that had no room for sentiment any more than kids or the institution of marriage, where assholes went after they were tired of being happy.

It was so easy to get caught up in the spectacle of kings, queens, and knights in shining armor. The mansion was many things, including a living history book, only without numbered pages to flip. All you had to do was walk and turn the corner. The rest was self-explanatory, regardless of who was doing the buying, selling, or bidding on the brass ring. Now toss in a bunch of really old, well-preserved things without the help of plastic surgeons, and Mr. Leach with his British accent and aristocratic mien, and you can see why I thought I was in another dimension, not only in time, but space.

Chapter Seven

All quests, large and small, begin with curiosity-ask any cat in Tin Pan Alley. Besides, how could I refuse to look into that window of Peeping Tom? How often is another world afforded us without booze, drugs, passports, or invitations to the Bohemian Club[35]? They say unless you venture beyond tourist traps, you are at the mercy of unscrupulous travel agents who will promise you the stars. During my excursions, I lost all sense of direction, of not only east and west, but right and wrong. Don't forget there were over a thousand halls and galleries in this Byzantine labyrinth.

But even when I got twisted around and disoriented, I was still afforded a wealth of information, not to mention one less wing to cross off my menu. Some rooms, especially on the first floor, were so warm that the heat had a presence like a tantalizing mirage in the Sahara Desert. Naturally, the more I snooped around the mansion, the more intimate nuances were revealed. Yet, even after four weeks and hundreds of elaborate hives, I still couldn't locate the portraits of Wolf, Frederick, or Salisbury. What gave me hope however was that I still had the fourth and fifth floors to explore. I knew they'd be up there-they had to be—but where? Still, it would leave the question: who was Mr. Leach in this whole sordid affair?

I began to vary the times of my stopovers in order to get a better overall perspective of Lord, Harry, and Gooseberry. Basically, I wanted to get a feel for the place after normal business hours in the event I had to make a late night visit. All the while, I had to keep up the appearance that these were social callings and not some juggler's windfall. Mr. Leach didn't mind these late night intrusions. If anything, he seemed to encourage them because it gave him more alone time with me, and in a different light, one only afforded after sunset.

Just as during the day, these nighttime forays began with the Gombahs, but inevitably, Mr. Leach veered off onto another road that had neither address nor milestone. After a while, it seemed as if he was just paying The Boys' lip service before focusing his attentions exclusively upon me. I really don't know if I was ever actually afraid of Mr. Leach, but to tell you the truth, I was never totally comfortable alone with him either. And I had a gun and badge.

One night after drinks in the Eden Room, Mr. Leach asked, "What I would give to keep my perfect record intact?" To this day, I can still hear his fiendish words burrowing into my ears. I really didn't know how else to respond. I mean, I did, but I didn't. I was caught off guard by the sudden audacity of the question. I quickly disarmed the awkward pause with a sarcastic response of "a left pinky and a right nut."

Although my attempt at gutter humor fell on deaf ears, Mr. Leach was serious as a heart attack. My evasiveness neither sidetracked nor deterred him. If anything, it reinvigorated him with a different avenue of approach that basically asked the same thing, only in more subtle, roundabout terms of insinuation and innuendo. Still, I was curious how this old man could bring such wishes to fruition? Was he a sorcerer?—A warlock?—A time traveler? Or was he just looking to plea bargain and turn State's evidence on somebody else? With Mr. Leach, it was always and forever multiple choice.

Despite these late night sojourns, Mr. Leach was still crisp, fluid, and lucid, showing not a hint of slowing down. His guard, as well as his head, was never lowered, not even for an instant. He had a readiness about him day or night to not only buy, but sell. He was forever ready to deal with someone for something. He said, "A chance isn't what you get, a chance is what you take." He was like Monty Hall, only with an edge and a thousand doors to choose from.

Mr. Leach, like the mansion, was chock full of surprises. It was osmosis, a rubbing off from one old thing to another. Little did I realize at the time of my tarriances, how prophetic that assessment would turn out to be. I never met a man who could counter my every move without a shyster on retainer choreographing their every legal dance step. It was almost as if Mr. Leach had access to my playbook.

"Wisdom derives from the experience before the experience. It comes not as a sheep to be sheared, but a king amongst kings to be crowned. That's why they gauge a fighter's fists and biceps—because they can't measure his heart and soul," Mr. Leach professed during one of his closing arguments that always capped our late night conversations.

I knew I was never going to outflank Mr. Leach under these convoluted, home field conditions. But if I couldn't get a change of venue, I would need another plan of attack. But even this would become a moot point when Mr. Leach informed me one evening that he was soon going abroad, with no date confirmed for his return to the Colonies, as he still liked to call the United States. Needless to say, this greatly changed and accelerated the dynamics of my investigative timetable. What made matters worse was I had nothing, absolutely nothing to prevent or even stall him from leaving the country.

How could I make a case in the name of the law when I didn't have anything to even get a search warrant to prospect for incriminating documents or bills of sale, which, at Lord, Harry, and Gooseberry, were always final? Mr. Leach once told me, during one of our fireside chats, that every transaction was documented and warehoused in the mansion's underground storage facilities. It, however, wasn't just the docu-drop for the Manhattan branch, but every satellite auction house of Lord, Harry, and Gooseberry around the world. Fortunately, I was present during several of these Fed Ex special deliveries to the mansion. And each time, without fail, the filing cabinets were huddled and stacked right outside that door labeled "Employees Only." What lied on the other side of that bigoted door? More importantly, how could I get behind it without court orders or civil lawsuits?—Or without being seen? That was a horse of a very different color that couldn't be found on any chart of bookies or handicappers at Belmont[36].

Don't get me wrong, I was a good cop who went by the Blue Book[37], but only as a reference point. You have to understand, when you're in the streets, you're the final arbiter between twelve jurors and six pallbearers. My corruptions, however, were constrained to looking where I wasn't supposed to be looking. Plainview doctrines and search warrants were at times mere technicalities to me. If the bad guys could break the rules, why couldn't I at least bend them? To my credit, I never stretched the truth and then called a tailor, nor did I ever plant or fabricate evidence to make a case. Something to live for should be the same thing you're willing to die for. Still, I have to admit I was quite a crackerjack lock picker; doors, safes, windows, and of course, mouths. I figured if all else failed, I could at least become a cat burglar. That's how fine the distinction is between cops and robbers.

I still didn't know who or what I was actually dealing with here. There were so many points of contention. But I knew man, just as luck, could only be good or bad. Sure I had my hunches and suspicions, but where one line of inference ended, another quickly picked up the slack of conjecture, and in an entirely different direction. I wasn't about to consider listening to common sense any more than those voices of better angels. I was out there all alone without a *maybe* to my *so*. I couldn't help it any more than change it. I found partners boring, parochial, and forever condemned to thinking inside the box. Another thing, they never saw those telltale signs of jilted lovers who always wanted the last word before the final curtain. To me, criminal investigations, like voyages of self-discovery, were solo enterprises, a Lindbergh if you will, that had no co-pilots, sidekicks, or Dr. Watson's in tow. Besides, that safety in numbers bullshit never really appealed to me, which is why, to this day, I have only two words to say on the subject: Kitty Genovese[38].

What I also found somewhat peculiar was why anyone, especially a man of Mr. Leach's intelligence, would store his most valuable documents by a furnace room in the basement. Paper and fire are never conducive to happy endings, regardless of who's writing the story. I chalked it up to just another British quirk. There were many oddities and irregularities about Lord, Harry, and Gooseberry that defied both logic and explanation. And just when I thought I had seen it all, I came face to face with the life-sized portraits of Wolf, Frederick, and Salisbury in a fifth floor rogues gallery. There was no mistake about it. Their taxonomic surnames were arrogantly displayed right beneath their gold framed racks. This was no longer about coincidences, time warps, or superstitions. Now it was about making the connection to Mr. Leach.

Chapter Eight

For several successive nights after that bomb was dropped, I studiously watched the foot traffic in, out, and around the mansion. I was trying to see if a pattern might develop, one that would present the least amount of resistance to my after-hours activities. After all, it was one thing to break into the mansion, it was quite another to break in without being detected and seen. I knew I couldn't just prance through the front door and stroll through the place. I needed a way, both secluded and close to that basement portal. What I was really looking for, however, was a shortcut beyond the jugular to the carotid artery. I should point out that every time I visited Lord, Harry, and Gooseberry, I was channeled into the Main Hall. You might say it was my port of entry. And even with my special guest privileges, I could still only go where Mr. Leach wanted me to go. In essence, I was seeing what he wanted me to see.

Needless to say, this left many voids, particularly in regards to the lower levels. To combat my sub-strata shortcoming, I was able to procure a blueprint from the Recorder of Deeds at City Hall. The old blueprint of the mansion circa 1893 revealed several considerable wine cellars as well as a dozen or more subordinate basement chambers that plunged to depths up to and including three hundred yards.

All my subsequent plans now pivoted on finding a secluded opening and when it would be made available to me. Still, I knew I just couldn't march in like a storm trooper. There were other urgent matters that had to be addressed. Chiefly, would there be security guards or nighttime custodians on the premises? I had to take these and other pertinent concerns into consideration. This was far from being a cake walk in Central Park with a pooper scooper. I recalled Mr. Leach saying he didn't want to disturb the integrity of the historic mansion by installing freight elevators. That little nugget of information was fine by me, since the last thing you want is to draw any unnecessary attention to yourself on a B and E[39]. Besides, anything that makes noise at night is magnified tenfold.

I had to do many things on the fly now. I couldn't take my sweet time waiting for perfection to inspire me. Mr. Leach did say he would soon be leaving, and although "soon" is open to a host of interpretations, I situated it on the short end of that tenured stick, which further expedited my activities both in and out of the mansion.

I went on several reconnoitering missions inside the mansion. I had to check for closed-circuit cameras, heat and light sensors, motion detectors, and electronic trip-wires. Oddly, no security devices were found, not even on the first floor, which, if you recall, extended from Pearl Street to the Avenue of the Finest. Who knows, maybe it was an unspoken rule, a kind of honor among thieves. All I know is that I had never seen so many treasures exposed to smash and grab tactics. Unless, of course, there was something else that didn't register and catch my roving eye. That was a very distinct possibility, one that made me apprehensive and extremely edgy. What I can see, I can handle; it's the unseen that's the silent killer.

None of the windows on the first floor had shutters or burglar bars either. Only public access doors and mandatory fire escape exits had any sort of advanced locking mechanisms to prohibit unwanted entry. To tell you the truth, the only thing missing was a flashing neon sign that said "Welcome." The mansion was that inviting. The only reason I could surmise for this breach of security was that Lord, Harry, and Gooseberry was a historic city landmark in a densely populated urban area. What other explanation could there possibly be?

Honestly, I'd seen dilapidated flophouses in the Bronx with more protective bells and whistles. Even without these egregious oversights, this gravitational field was much too powerful to resist with token resistance. Curiosity was consuming me, propelling me, driving me ever the more closer to that line of discretion that's never to be crossed by trespassers or non-union scabs. However, if I didn't heed fatherly advice to be careful, why on earth would I now be obliged to follow proper police procedure?

Through no fault of my own, I had become the man who skips work to play a round of golf, and just as he couldn't speak about an incredible hole-in-one without blowing his cover, neither could I spill my guts without implicating myself in what I was about to undertake.

To top it all off, I didn't even know who or what I was specifically looking for to validate my outrageous claims. In my entire police career, I'd never done anything so reckless and rash. Yet there I was, poised on the brink of my own self-destruction, awaiting a dark night to carry me over the threshold.

Sure, I was trying to prove something criminally, but I was also trying to prove something to myself as well as the world at large. After all, it's not the 2665 cases I solved, but the one I couldn't crack. I didn't want to be defined by that one monumental failure. But how could I not? Crimes of the Century make or break careers. They forever typecast and crystallize you at that specific moment in time. Yet there I was, pandering to suspicions and gut instincts while prowling around in the shadows, looking for a weakness to exploit. If it wasn't so pathetic, it would have been tragic to have everything including my stellar record riding on a flight of fancy.

It doesn't exactly breed confidence when your best hunches are running around in bell towers.

Never had my faith been put to the litmus test. Sure, I believed in God, a Sunday God, one I got all dressed up to go visit once a week at St. Daniel's. To me, church was nothing but a rendezvous point for hypocrites who were only religious about going there at the same time every Sunday. When I was growing up, it seemed like just another Italian controlled racket, only you surrendered allowance money for protection from a Bogeyman who didn't carry a blackjack and stiletto.

Chapter Nine

My last official meeting with Mr. Leach, after gathering all the pertinent facts, was not only different in manner, but tone. Maybe I caught him at a bad time. Why else would he be so blunt and adversarial? I sensed not only hostility for my presence, but contempt in the mere mention of my name. Before, I was John, but now I was banished to "Detective."

Mr. Leach was never before deliberately rude to me. His shortness of diplomacy was so out of his refined character. A rejected suitor had more civil refinement after being discarded to that scrap heap of broken hearts. I knew something was amiss when he didn't even want to discuss the Gombahs. Was he perhaps reading my body language, or worse, my mind? Maybe I had just worn out my welcome. But this was not a contempt founded on over-familiarity. This one hundred and eighty degree turn stemmed from something I didn't yet know or contractually understand. Either way, I was taken completely aback because Mr. Leach was, if not gracious with his time, at least tolerant when I unexpectedly infringed upon it.

To get anything out of Mr. Leach now, including his departure time and date, was a struggle on par with pulling hen's teeth. Every answer he supplied was in concise, measured monotones. Why he bothered to see me that day is still a mystery. It was difficult to ignore the slight, it really was, but I knew I had to stay in character and act as if nothing was going on behind the scenes. It's one thing to stoke a man's ire; it's another to arouse his misgivings.

Before departing, Mr. Leach cryptically informed me that people who betrayed him "only did so once." Why he left me with that tenebrous bon mot[40] I can only hazard a guess. But as with everything else, there was a host of reasons. In the final analysis, however, there were only two possibilities to actively consider; they either became friends, or the person was killed. As strange as it sounds, it was only the day before that Mr. Leach said, "Opportunity, as death, knocks on the same door." For my sake, I was just hoping it didn't say "Employees Only."

I now awaited a cloudy, overcast sky that masked the waxing gibbous[41]. I wanted every possible advantage I could get, because if my premises were correct, I was going to need more than a couple of Our Fathers and Hail Marys.

As Luck or Fate or God would have it, the night I chose was rain-filled with claps of thunder to intermittently applaud my hesitant footfalls. One of the drawbacks of a city that never sleeps is the inordinate amount of people out at all crazy hours. So not only did I have to dodge pelting raindrops and streetlights, I also had to avoid prowling car beams and drunken Friday night revelers hopping from one smoky bistro and cabaret to the next.

I had discovered an out-of-the-way fire escape exit on the south side of the original mansion off Pearl Street to be the most isolated as well as the closest to the basement door. Still, it would be a nice little jaunt that had no direct route. Without incident, I picked the deadbolt and, despite a shrill squeak from the rusty hinges, I quickly entered and hushed the door behind me.

At this time, I didn't require the use of my mag-light due to the heavenly paparazzi with their brilliant flashes. This light show more or less became my guide across those vulcanized floors that instantly evaporated any moisture shed by my retentive gym shoes. I zigzagged through majestic halls, grand ballrooms, and elongated corridors. Never had I moved so hesitantly or cautiously toward a goal. The only thing I could hear, besides bitch slaps of Mother Nature, was my heart furiously pounding like a migraine in a kettledrum.

After several intense minutes, I was dismissed into a narrow hallway freckled by quivering candles. I was never more afraid than I was now in this claustrophobic channel that had no nooks or crannies to dart into if someone happened to approach. I molested and groped the walls so much I couldn't avoid that unwanted connection to a goddamn wallflower.

How is it that everything seems so much more distant and far away in the dark? Halls and galleries that were effortlessly negotiated during the day were now holes in my resume. I couldn't be sure, but the mansion didn't seem like the same place. In a way, it reminded me of the forest preserves that take on a whole other character after nightfall.

The mansion was more portentous now too, giving no quarter to crumb-less fools who lost their way in the dark. Despite that elusive smell being the same, the soundtrack was decidedly different from the one that entertained the day.

Fireplaces, although raging with renewed vigor and energy, strangely gave off very little light. It was weird, as if the flames were specialized to their immediate vicinity. I could never quite shake that feeling of trepidation or those attentive eyes of Argus[42] that watched my every step through portrait galleries that never seemed to end. The violent thunderstorm raging outside was a perfect complement to the ghoulishness of the old and dead inside the mansion. It was creepy, a horror flick come to life, only the totality of it all was much greater than its parts, regardless of who played them to the hilt.

Finally, I came upon that "Employees Only" door just beyond the lavish Eden Room. The door was inviting, yet forbidding all at once. So ambivalent it had become. This was no longer a moment of truth, but a million moments all rolled into one throw of the dice. I momentarily paused with a sense of both relief and dread; relief for having located my prize, and dread for having to now peek behind the wizard's curtain. In an odd way, it seemed easy—too easy—and although that was my intention, it seemed like it was someone else's too.

Slowly, cautiously, I turned the knob and eased open the heavy, gold door. Only instead of seeing a single declining set of stairs, there was another extended hallway bleeding into scores of partisan stairwells that all fled downward at various angles and rates of descent.

What came as a total surprise also came with a perplexing question: which one to choose? How do you plot a course in uncharted waters? The blueprint wasn't just outdated; it was obsolete in every sense of the word. This was one time that old wasn't the best in existence. I should point out that these were not your typical, conventional stairwells of paint, plaster, and sixty watt bulbs dangling from cobwebbed ceilings. It was far from it. These were eight foot high and wide holes bored right into the earth with countless granite stairs that had no evenness or regulated breadth of step. There were no electric outlets either. The only source of light was provided by pudgy candles carved into stone recesses, which limited their dispersal to retarded puddles.

If this were a coin toss, my decision would have been a slam dunk. The selection process, however, was far from being rendered so academic. With several dozen stairwells to choose from, ranging from double-zero to ninety-nine, my choices were a little more complicated than the youthful fickleness of Eenie, Meenie, Minie, Mo.

All the stairwells retreated downward, but some were at such radical and severe inclines that they could be construed as mine shafts rather than flights of stairs. I slowly worked my way down the dim corridor momentarily pausing by each and every opening and listened for the distinct pitter patter of man. Every stairwell belched a thermal, dry heat that made the candles frolic and dance with foreboding shadows. From every aperture, I could also hear a continuous rumbling and murmur. Whether it was from man or machine, I couldn't readily discern one way or another. How far down it was coming from couldn't be determined either.

I decided to take stairwell ninety-two for no other apparent reason than it was quieter than the others I had auscultated[43]. As I began my canary descent, it was getting gradually and noticeably warmer. This condition only increased as I went further and further down. After an hour or so, it got so warm that I had to discard some of my outer garments to tolerate the stifling heat. How was this possible? Getting good and sweaty with granite entombed all around me defied physics.

The plummeting stairs kept taking me further and further down. I knew I had traveled more than three hundred yards. How far, exactly, I can only surmise. It was safe to say it was a lot further than nine hundred feet. Being an avid runner, with five New York City marathons under my belt, I knew when I got rumors of shin splints that I was well over a mile in distance. Still, there was no sign of a wine cellar, boiler room, or underground storage facility. I kept thinking I took the wrong stairwell. Yet, for some inexplicable reason, I continued to go down that ghastly wormhole that had no apparent end in sight.

The mysterious stench that reeked on Mr. Leach had its origins in this root cellar. That's when it finally dawned on me. This was the sulfurous odor I detected that night at the Gombahs' penthouse. But as one riddle of the Sphinx was solved, a hundred more were added to the ever-growing list of panderers, pimps, used car salesmen, and hypocrites.

I moved at a brisk clip from the pronounced grade and downward momentum of gravity, but always within the strict parameters of a rhythmic pace. I knew I had to maintain a disciplined gait not only to conserve energy, but to control the amount of noise. The stairwell acted as a conduit and echo chamber so out of necessity I had to be as inconspicuous as possible in regards to sound and light dispersal. Although meager and spotty, the stocky candles were sufficient to illuminate the immediate foreground so no guesswork was involved in the process of putting one foot in front of the other.

Just when I was beginning to doubt my sanity and question where these stairs were leading, they drained into a huge, gouged cavern half a mile long and maybe half that high and across. After being confined in a narrow tube, I felt reborn. The truly amazing thing about this cavern, however, were the mobs of filing cabinets circumnavigating it from ceiling to floor. There had to be forty to fifty million, maybe more. I'd never seen a storage facility quite like this before. It was on an epic, no, colossal scale, not only in regards to the sheer volume of filing cabinets, but the amount of time and energy required to not only fill this cavern up, but to create it in the first place. Evidently, faith and dynamite aren't the only things to move mountains.

I was overwhelmed by the enormity of it all. It's not every day you stumble upon a Wonder of the World. I wanted to capture the moment on my cell phone, but the heat had damaged and melted it so much I couldn't even turn it on. I didn't know how or where to begin. The amount of difficulty in finding the Gombahs' filing cabinet down here was located somewhere between you-got-to-be-kidding-me and are-you-fucking-nuts? Sure, I was disappointed. I never expected this development. An eternal optimist would have been crestfallen and knocked to his knees. It was staggering any which way you looked at it, whether you were searching for someone or not.

I didn't even know if I was in the right storage facility. Seriously, how many more underground storage chambers could there possibly be? I couldn't help but think about what I got myself into. However, it was too late to cut and run, especially when I had nothing to implicate Mr. Leach in the three Gombahs' deaths. It was now or never for me to connect the dots back to him. There was no denying that any more than scavenging for dirt to salvage my spotless reputation.

I browsed and grazed where my hungers and acquired tastes drove me. These gluttonous pursuits were really nothing more than a potluck approach to see what my eyes could feast upon next. With each and every file, it got easier until the obsession with dirty laundry became just another necessary evil to not feel bad about. It was perfect, almost ideal in the belief that something so calorically empty could be exclusively for me.

What's not to like about prying into illicit romances and illegal affairs? I gobbled pages and the knights they helped undress in front of me. Time restraints however hastened and put a damper on my meddlesome activities. I couldn't forget I had to be out of the mansion by the start of business, which at Lord, Harry, and Gooseberry's was 11 a.m. on Saturdays. So, I couldn't be a gossipy busybody if something wasn't inclusive to my witch hunt.

There were files in many languages dating back to 1092, a lot of good that did me. One of my regrets is only being versed in English and Italian. I'm conversationally fluent in Spanish due to its etymological romance with my Latin roots. Their written language, with its feminine and masculine nuances, did have a tendency of eluding me on occasion. That, however, was more of a stumbling block than a roadblock to understanding the meaning of a sentence. In that respect, I envied Mr. Leach and his gift of tongues. But his talent wasn't so much a redeeming quality as an expedient means to a contractual end.

I should inform you that everyone in this storage facility was deceased, even those from 1992, which was the latest year I was able to ascertain. Now stairwell ninety-two made sense; it was all the calendar years ending in the digits ninety-two. There was apparently no rhyme or reason to the filing system employed down here, at least not any I could visibly discern. It wasn't so much intentionally haphazard as it was organized chaos. Maybe closed files no longer had to be alphabetized or numerically dated and sequenced. The thought did cross my mind. How diametrically opposed was this Chinese fire drill from upstairs where everything was meticulously ranked, categorized, and catalogued by noble birth. It was hard to believe this was the same business, but roots look nothing like the fruits they nourish and give life to; for as one sucks, the other looks for suckers.

Inside the rusty filing cabinets, the mayhem was no different. It was a hodgepodge of contracts, bills of sale, personal artifacts, and other everyday paraphernalia found in a man's desk. Travelogues, expense accounts, business journals, and diaries were the most conspicuous and prevalent of dusty possessions. What really caught my attention was the careless, almost reckless manner in which these files were signed, sealed and delivered to this junkyard in Lower Manhattan. To me, it seemed as if the contents were rifled through before being dumped pell-mell into these metal tombs. The overall impression I got was a rush job of one drawer being hurriedly and unceremoniously emptied into another by someone who didn't give a damn about decorum any more than final contractual dispositions.

CHAPTER TEN

Despite a circuitous proliferation of fluttering torches freckled around the cavern, I still had to utilize my flashlight. Reading by flashlight, although adequate in terms of getting the job done, is very tedious and strenuous. I also had to be on guard for my safety, I was, after all, trespassing on private property. I had to be cognizant of this, regardless what else I was doing. The last thing I wanted was to get pinched, or worse, shot by some trigger happy, minimum wage security guard. My concentration level was further diffused by sulfur-filled air stinging my watery eyes.

A continuous characteristic of every filing cabinet was the Lord, Harry, and Gooseberry contracts. What made them unique, however, is that they were all drawn up and signed in a very unique and distinct red ink not found on any known color chart. Maybe this was just another patented trademark of Lord, Harry, and Gooseberry, like the Red Trident. I must admit, I wasn't paying much attention to specific legalese or first and second party ramifications pertaining to Contract Law. My focus, like I said, was centered exclusively upon the Gombahs and trying to find documents tying Mr. Leach to their deaths. That was the reasoning behind my myopia[44] to see what I wanted to see while disregarding the rest. But that's just how it is when you're single-minded of purpose with blinders on.

After several hours and hundreds of files, I decided to broaden my dragnet to include anything and everything from extortion and blackmail letters to compromising photographs. I was now trolling the bottom of every filing cabinet looking for something, anything, to justify my claims of Buyer Beware.

I also began reading more into those contracts with their qualifying offers and special once-in-a-lifetime conditional guarantees. Provisions were ironclad, unyielding, and different, very different from any found on standard business agreements. Many were the clauses that had Santa attached but without any reference to Jesus, Mary, and Joseph, or a manure infested manger in Bethlehem.

The contracts were straightforward and airtight with no loopholes, Houdini escape provisions, or money back guarantees. Trappings with all the greed breed fixings could be updated for the contractual duration of terms that coincidently ranged anywhere from twelve to twenty-one to twenty-five to fifty years. However, there could be no changes or modifications in regards to one's final arraignment, which was basically nothing more than an old twist on a new arm.

Evidently, Lord, Harry, and Gooseberry were more than big time sellers; they were also big game buyers. But what exactly did they purchase? Over the years, it's had many names, many monikers: The Essence, The Well of Being, The Unseen Thing, God's Gift, and The Immortal Coil. Many are the aliases of The Devil's Due!

Even after absorbing this hellish truth, I was momentarily frozen in terror and disbelief. How could this be? How could this possibly be? Father Mike was right; the Devil was in the Big Apple. Sure, I toyed with the idea, but that was really more of a Catholic fantasy than anything else.

Why I didn't run out of there after this hellish revelation, I still can't fully rationalize or explain. Was it because there was no Statute on the books in New York about buying and selling souls? Was it perhaps the apostate seeking redemption? Or was it the little kid inside me looking for indisputable evidence to nail the killer of his boyhood idols? Who knows? Regardless of my motive, how often is one given an opportunity of this magnitude? Sure, I was scared shitless. What sane man wouldn't be? I was not only in the Devil's element, I was in his Lair. And although I was in deep, I knew I had to go deeper to find my Eurydice[45].

Bravery and stupidity are identical twins; don't let anyone tell you any differently. When I should have been heading back to the surface, I decided to stay and play twenty questions with myself, starting with, "When there's hell to pay, who's the broker?"

In all probability, my gung-ho bravado would've been short lived if I didn't stumble across a yawning gash at the far end of the catacomb. At first, I was hesitant to deviate from the Devil I knew, or thought I did from twelve years of Catholic school. But since I'd come this far, what was the sense of being bashful now? Besides, I wanted out of this graveyard. And all the while, I thought that dust in the filing cabinets was a byproduct of this subterranean environment.

This malefic rent[46] didn't lead to an adjoining storage chamber. Instead, it fled into another bottomless flight of stairs that had no apparent end in sight. I believe even if I wanted to turn around I couldn't. Some unseen force was now pulling me further down into this entombing darkness where a jealous miasma[47] stubbornly clung to the caustic air. Soon, the earthen pitch got so radical that I was hurled in a free fall spiral at nearly three times my normal gait. It was getting so oppressively hot I had to discard my Rolex as if it was stolen from a wise guy from Five Points[48]. With each and every step in this sweltering cauldron, the gripping heat was getting more relentless. I wasn't just hemorrhaging, I was slowly melting away.

Several times I had to resort to wringing hot, briny sweat from my t-shirt just to moisten my cracked lips. It got so intense at times

I could barely muster enough spit to soothe my cotton mouth. Everything everywhere was parched and desiccated. The narrow stairwell trapped heat as if it too were a prisoner of convective circumstances.

What further prolonged my agony and suffering was that I couldn't sit on stairs or lean against walls for comfort or repose. Everything in, on, and around me that could conduct heat was smoldering and blistering to the touch. I couldn't even stand in one place longer than a few seconds before my rubber soles started heating up.

Was ego or revenge spurring me on, or was I simply being lured and stuffed further down into this Chimney of Gehenna[49]? I could no more stop that thought than help myself in preventing this from happening to me.

Laments, once distant and ill defined, were now resonating with definition and certainty that could no longer be denied. The dialogue of eternal damnation and endless human suffering hauntingly ricocheted throughout the soniferus[50] stairwell. Suddenly, it was a madhouse of horrifying screams and spine curdling cries that could no longer be masked, ignored, or attributed to something else brewing further down below.

The funnel of granite mercifully spilled into another immense vault, only this one wasn't bloated with hordes of filing cabinets, but rather a riot of gold. I had never seen anything like it. I was like Ali Baba, only this Aladdin's Cave was not some young bride's bedroom fantasy. This was the real deal, the mother of all mother lodes.

Everywhere I looked, there were gold bricks. And all were incused with the Red Trident, patent trademark of Lord, Harry, and Gooseberry. I must clarify something for you. I'm not talking about piles, stacks, or even mounds of gold; I'm talking about mountains, mountains of gold!

The gold entombed here would have not just flooded markets, it would've drowned them. Fort Knox was but a footnote compared to this Mint of Juno[51]. The endless accumulation and surplus dwarfed every king's wealth in the known world. Not even a man's wildest dreams could have conjured this Underworld Treasury. The monotony never lost its allure or fascination with me. That's the truly magical thing about gold—it never loses its luster and shine, whether recently panned or a thousand years old.

I wanted to take a bar, but not only was it scalding, it was condensed and heavy, maybe sixty to seventy pounds. And in my withering physical condition, I had to decline the temptation. Remember, I still had miles of stairs to negotiate, along with the fact that gravity would not be aiding and abetting my escape.

Even as I walked slack-jawed through this Mine of Golconda[52], I kept thinking how I was going to book all this gold into evidence. It would take an army of men years. The Evidence Custodian would have a fucking heart attack. Strange how the mind works, but I kept insisting on applying rules from a world that no longer had meaning, merit, or precedence.

Although the scale and scope of my investigation had dramatically changed, my target remained the same. I knew, however, I would need something more to make my case besides some bloody contracts. I needed something indisputable, not only to prove my case, but to close down this lurid Sweatshop.

I was totally captivated and spellbound until I happened upon a suggestive orifice to which, needless to say, I was automatically now drawn. I couldn't help myself anymore. Self restraint, like the dodo, was gone. All I knew was I had to have a look inside. Even the condemned fool has to ask, how could I refuse? Still, I had to entertain the thought: was this pre-ordained or pre-meditated as a mouse trap with cheese? But instead of another flight of bottomless stairs, I was deposited into a feverish little grotto that was very intimate in commemorative detail and tuft hunting design.

Immediately, I noticed many haunting parallels to a serial killer's parlor where souvenirs of victims are kept close at hand to be fondled, treasured, and masturbated over. The only thing was these keepsakes and mementos were all top drawer, even without a bureau to determine their select vintage and pecking order.

Beyond an old portrait of the three Gombahs on the granite wall when they were little devils growing up, the décor was wanting and sparse. There wasn't even a rickety chair in this steamy cave, or anything else for that matter, to take a load off your feet. There were filing cabinets here, but nothing to threaten the numerical superiority of crypt lot ninety-two. But if names were unknown and inconsequential before, they were now what you might call historically renowned. They were immediately recognized by one name and one name alone: Napoleon, Stalin, Hitler, Washington, Galileo, Shakespeare, Caesar, Ferdinand, and Isabella.

Whereas their portraits were worth a thousand words in the Gallery of Souls, down here an entirely different story was being told from the one schoolboys recited as gospel in those temples of higher learning.

I opened the polished filing cabinet on Ferdinand and Isabella first because it was closest to me. Inside the metal sarcophagus I found two ornate gold crowns, two bejeweled scepters, three glass vials containing gray ash, and a leather-bound book written by a man named Cristobal Colon. For a moment, I was taken aback and perplexed until I recalled Christopher Columbus was just the Anglicized version of the famous Italian explorer's name. But how did his journal get put into King Ferdinand and Queen Isabella's filing cabinet?

When I opened the Journal, a wizened leaf aimlessly fluttered to the ground at my feet. What was the purpose of this leaf amongst leaves of a different tree? Hurriedly, I retrieved the amaranth[53] and wedged it firmly back between the cover and frontispiece[54] where it was originally concealed as a sentimental reminder to another past conquest of Paradise. The Journal was written in Castilian Spanish and, every so often, sprinkled with Italian words and phrases. I should point out that Castilian Spanish is not a very economical language, yet for some unexplainable reason, Columbus chose it as his literary medium. Not only did the book look and feel different, it also read different. Before I proceed, I should point out that I have not distorted or embellished the integrity of the text. The passages of Columbus, along with his hopes, dreams, and cautions, remain intact along with those cauterized dates incused upon my photographic memory banks. I began at the beginning.

6 June 1492

My travels have taken me from Portugal to Rome and now to Spain. I am hoping the third time will be a charm. I can only pray someone will sponsor my dream. Neither the King of Portugal nor Pope Alexander agreed with the opinion that the world is round. Pope Alexander warned me, saying he would not be party to such blasphemies. His Holiness told me if I persisted in my heresies he would have me placed under house arrest. How can people be so blind? How can you behold the sun and moon and still believe the world is flat? Thankfully, when in Rome, I found a sympathetic ally in Cardinal DeMore, confessor and spiritual adviser to the Court in Aragon. Cardinal DeMore has arranged for me to present my maps and charts to King Ferdinand and Queen Isabella of Spain. We embarked a fortnight ago for San Sebastian on the Virgin Queen, a tidy vessel with a good reputation, a well-seasoned crew, and a God fearing Captain.

9 June 1492

When I arrived at the Court in San Sebastian, I didn't know what to expect. Not only was I granted immediate audience, but the royal couple was open to the idea of the world being round. Not only that, but they believed in my ability to prove it. Acting in concert and speaking as one, King Ferdinand said they would sponsor my voyage, fully financing and outfitting three vessels, the decked ship Santa Maria, and two caravels, the Nina and the Pinta. All three vessels will fly under the Spanish gonfalon[55] with me as Captain upon the Santa Maria. I don't know how to thank Cardinal DeMore. All he asks in return is for me to include his old friend, the navigator Angelo Marotte, aboard the Santa Maria. I told Cardinal DeMore I would extend the invitation first thing in the morning. How could I refuse his humble request? It also assists me, now I have an experienced helmsman on his Majesty's Flagship.

28 June 1492

I've been harassed for days by astrologers and cartographers. No one knows exactly what lies beyond the Pillars of Hercules[56]. Still, many hold to the old superstition as part of the Atlantic's legend. Many are my daily tasks of outfitting three ships with provisions, instruments, weapons, and two hundred men. There is little time for rest. I decided to set sail for Cathay[57] from Palos on the second of August. The Atlantic will be less prone to squalls. To many veteran Argonauts, it sounds absurd to travel west to get to the Great Khan in the East. If sanity were the yardstick for explorers, then man would still be living in caves.

31 July 1492

I have decided Martin Pinzon will command the Pinta while his brother, Vicente, will master the Nina. I could not have asked for two more competent and reliable sailors at the helms of his Majesty's ships. I have added Luis de Torres to the Santa Maria's manifest, due to his expertise on Eastern cultures and languages. He speaks several languages including Arabic, Chaldean, Mandarin, and Hebrew. My brothers Bartolome and Diego will accompany me on the Flagship. This will be the first time we have set sail since we were boys dreaming of distant and far away shores in Genoa.

1 August 1492

At dawn, we will set sail for the Canary Islands to pick up the trade winds. My anticipation will not allow an hour's respite. How often is one bestowed with the dream of a lifetime? Portugal rejected me, and Rome spurned and threatened me. It was only King Ferdinand and Queen Isabella who saw my vision and believed in me. It was as if the Royal Couple already had their minds made up before I even showed them my maps and charts. Cardinal DeMore, being Isabella's confessor and confidant, surely influenced their high opinion of me.

2 August 1492

We embarked Palos with little notice. That's how I wanted it. Our voyage is to remain a secret to discourage interlopers to my dream. Tonight I played several games of chess with the ship's spiritual adviser, Father Jude, a man of as many words as moves. He is a skilled player. No man ever bested me four times in one night. I like to think it was that extra glass of port after dinner. But the way the under-Secretary to Cardinal DeMore moved his royal pieces, he was a worthy adversary whether a man be sober or three sheets to the wind.

12 August 1492

We arrived in the Canary Islands. Not even Prince Henry the Navigator could match our speeds. I believe it is a new record. Never in my years at sea have I seen so accomplished a navigator as Angelo Marotte. The man is more vital than an astrolabe[58]*. I never witnessed a helmsman plot his course by dead reckoning alone. It is a remarkable talent. Marotte refuses to acknowledge the heavens for guidance, altogether neglecting and forsaking the sun, the moon and the stars. Still, he knows exactly where we are.*

27 September 1492

Good weather, bad weather, it rotates sometimes by the hour. It feels at times as if God is trying to deliberately discourage us from finding a Westward Passage to the Great Khan.

29 September 1492

Winds are capricious; one moment our sails are pregnant, the next they are still as a frightened cur. No sight of land or land birds. All we see are nomadic albatross and an endless ocean stretching into every horizon. The earth is either much bigger than my calculations or we will sail off the face of it. At this point, it can only be one of the other.

7 October 1492

The crew is easily agitated. Having not seen landfall for over a month has made many dark stories surface aboard the ship. There is even talk amongst the men about turning around. My brothers are of great assistance in reassuring the crew that we are on the right course and that God is on our side. Father Jude is also helpful in calming the men's fears with prayer and scripture. Father Jude reminds me that I am the Christ bearer, the earthly ambassador for King Ferdinand and Queen Isabella of Spain.

12 October 1492

Shortly after 2 a.m., Juan Barmejo from the prow of the Pinta sighted land. I immediately claimed the territory in the name of Spain and King Ferdinand and Queen Isabella. It is a great relief to know I was right all along and to finally be vindicated after all these years of ridicule and humiliation. But I couldn't have done it without Cardinal DeMore and Angelo Marotte, my tireless navigator. I have never seen so dedicated a sailor as Marotte. I have never seen the "Tall Spaniard," as the crew affectionately calls him, off the bridge. Any captain would petition to have such a sailor under his command. How blessed I have been. In the morning, we will walk upon land for the first time in almost two months. I can't wait.

I should briefly mention that it was very taxing to walk and read this clumsy book while simultaneously clutching my sizzling flashlight. I had no choice. I had to keep moving, like I said, to avoid the sting from a thermally heated undercarriage that scorched my feet if I stood in once place more than a few seconds. In those days, however, I was younger and more suited for the business of beating myself up. Besides, once I started reading about the Italian's National Hero, I was hooked. I have portaged over journal passages dealing with the inaugural landing as well as those dedications to God, King, and Country that accompany all flag planting ceremonies.

2 November 1492

Communication with the Arrowacki, as the indigenous savages are called, is difficult and time consuming. Angelo Marotte has shown a special talent for hammering out trade agreements while representing the Crown's vested interests. How quickly Marotte has learned to speak the savage's strange language. It has perplexed Torres, who still is at a loss for words. It feels as if we landed on the moon instead of a tropical paradise inhabited by naked savages. I must admit, I find their females enchanting. Father Jude assures me it's the vile remnants of a long voyage. Whatever it is, the attraction is real. The Arrowacki are a child-like people enraptured by playfulness and a direct simplicity in manner and speech. With the exception of modest trinkets in their noses and ears they wear or carry nothing else, not even weapons. The Arrowacki don't have a written language or words for such things as enemy or war. When I showed Chief Hooptalotto my weapons, he politely smiled before retiring to a neutral corner in his hut of thatch. The island of Arrowack is quite a departure from the Old World. In many ways, it's as refreshing as it is different. There is nothing modern here. It's almost as if the place has been frozen in time.

14 November 1492

Chief Hooptalotto and his many subjects have never heard of Cathay. Wherever we go throughout this archipelago we get the same quizzical look, the same shoulder shrug. No one seems to know its name, even as a giant gated land. We have traveled to several island groups and all are alike right down to their nakedness and innocence. The only thing these natives seem to wear are smiles and this they do proudly and unashamed. To be uniform without uniforms—what a novel approach. They show and give everything and hide nothing. They are at peace with abundance and prosperity without weapons, horses, or men in armor. I believe we are on the outer fringes of a vast mainland that stretches to Cathay. We are still in search of an interior passage that we hope will bring us to those Four Rivers of Paradise.

21 November 1492

Since hearing of the land where "gold is born" three days ago, the men have become sick with "yellow fever." To an extent, so have I. Father Jude has also been smitten. None of us can control ourselves. All we think and talk about is that magical land of El Dorado. Chief Hooptalotto says the Zuni who live in the Eighth City of Cibola are the children of the first beings in the World.

27 November 1492

It's been four days since we set sail. Our guide is Heawock, eldest son of Chief Hooptalotto. The young savage says we must travel by great waters for two more balls in Sky Court, then two more balls by land. We are anxious. None of us can sleep. We are all like Angelo Marotte now.

1 December 1492

We arrived in the Eighth City of Cibola this afternoon. It is a magnificent city that has no equal anywhere in the Old World. The City of Gold is truly a City of Gold. Everything from street gutters to rooftops is made of gold, not only in color, but the precious metal itself. It is a wondrous sight to behold. The city takes up the entire valley. It is a big valley, twenty leagues north and south and fifteen east to west. You could put the city of Rome in one section of this Valley and still have room for several more European cities. I am told that there are over a million savages living here. They also run around naked like the Arrowacki. There are well over half a million buildings, with some obtaining heights to rival our greatest European cathedrals. Their oral historians, the keepers and guardians of truth, tell me the Elder Race built the Eighth City of Cibola, according to their celestial reckoning, over five thousand years ago. The Eight Cities of Cibola, it is said, were built to eliminate man's lust for avarice and greed. One house here, even the smallest, could finance a flotilla, outfitting it with the finest nautical riggings, provisions, and weaponry. I am told the other Seven Cities are just as great as this one, only they are many, many balls away.

8 December 1492

Father Jude tries to baptize the Zuni. The savages here, as elsewhere, refuse to abandon their ancestral gods which Heawock informs me are as numerous as the stars. The savages only want to incorporate Jesus into their pantheon. I know Father Jude gets angry, but only as a stern father with a wayward son. He remains determined to break the savages of their pagan ways. He tells me their watery isolation has blinded them to the light. He maintains the New World savages are the lost tribe of Israel. How, though, did they arrive here? Those crudely crafted canoes that litter their sandy shoes could not have carried them across the Atlantic. When I brought this to Father Jude's attention, he said, "God works in mysterious ways." But if that were true, how is it their oral historians don't have any knowledge of a trans-Atlantic crossing? Something so important and life changing would surely warrant mention.

12 December 1492

Bad news! I was informed shortly after midnight by Heawock that a boo-boo happened to Juan Barmejo and Angelo Marotte on the outskirts of the city. A local Zuni said a fire serpent devoured Juan Barmejo. Angelo Marotte, who was with Barmejo moments earlier, has also vanished without a trace. I will travel to the location in the morning.

13 December 1492

When I arrived at the site this morning, all I saw was a clump of ash that an old savage said was once Juan Barmejo. When I inquired to the fate of Angelo Marotte, the old savage said, "He slithered like beast with no legs into jungle." With superstitious savages, it's difficult to tell what actually happened and what they really saw. There were two distinct sets of footprints in the soft soil leading to this clearing, but none afterwards. It was as if both men just vanished. I formed two search parties to scour the surrounding villages and jungle for Barmejo and Marotte. Martin Pinzon led one party into the surrounding villages while I, along with twenty men and fifteen savages, entered the great jungle where we now camp for the night. God help us.

16 December 1492

The jungle is dense and overcrowded with heat, noise, and insects of every color, size and shape. The thick canopy suffocates and filters sunshine. In the middle of the day, it sometimes feels like midnight. There have been no sign of Marotte or Barmejo for three days now. I cannot help but fear the worst. I owe it to both men to continue the search for another day or two before returning to El Dorado.

17 December 1492

The Zuni can go anywhere throughout this great jungle and not only survive, but thrive. Never before have I seen people so in touch with the land. They have struck a perfect balance with nature. Now I know why nothing has changed here in over five thousand years. Their lives stress harmony and togetherness. In the jungle, everything from food to medicine can be found and in endless abundance. I never thought eating bark from a tree could cure a man of indigestion. There are remedies and cures in the great jungle for every ailment and sickness that inflicts the Zuni. There are plants in the jungle to not only energize the eyes but strengthens a weak heart. There is indeed magic at work here, but I don't know what it is. All I know is that it's good magic, one that helps and provides for the savages. Virtually every tree in the jungle supports some sort of nourishment or cure. There is definitely more to the Zuni than what I initially assumed.

18 December 1492

I've officially concluded the search for Barmejo and Marotte. I hope the other search party has been more successful. We will be returning to the City of Gold tomorrow.

21 December 1492

Three days it has rained. I've never seen skies so foreboding and black. It is as if hell has revisited the heavens. I've never witnessed Mother Nature cry like this before. Our speed has been greatly hampered. Our clothes are soaked, which only further restricts our movement. Our European dress is so excessive and out of place compared to the savages who run around naked in the rain. The Zuni and Arrowacki don't have words for many things, including greed and murder. They are content to know paradise and be part of its never ending ball. It is a world turned upside down only without a frown on their red washed, cherubic faces.

25 December 1492

We re-entered the Eighth City of Cibola on Christmas Day. What a gift! With the sky free of rain, I had to squint. The city was brighter than the silver seas at noontime. It is nice to be back amongst the savages who are so trusting and accessible. They ask for nothing but our company and give us anything we desire and want; they cannot say no. I don't think there is a word for it in their vocabulary. What a refreshing change; they have no political intrigue or hidden agendas. The Zuni don't have locks on their windows or doors. Everything is open, especially their arms, which they embrace me with every chance they get. The Zuni have no laws for rape or robbery. Their oral historians don't even have words to give meaning or expression to those vile acts. What the Zuni have in lieu of laws are rules of good conduct as a guest would have at a host's dinner table. This is what governs and rules their actions with friends, family, and strangers. The city elders provide the only recognizable form of government. It is done without enforcement or Salic[59] *standards that one must obey or else. Each and every savage is a willing participant in this social covenant. There is no slavery or subjection by the strong over the old and weak. Everything down to the smallest detail is done out of love and respect, not fear and intimidation that is so emblematic in the Old World. Commerce is brisk and active in and beyond the Valley. With gold so profuse, it is rendered worthless as a bargaining instrument. It is considered bad manners and an insult to offer it in exchange for something else, including a bag of beans. Its abundance has deflated its market value to where it's sheer madness to kill for or die over. Since there is no written language throughout the land everything from traditions to trade is orally passed along from father to son so no misunderstandings can occur with words that have no loving tongue.*

P.S. Before retiring for the evening, Martin Pinzon informed me Juan Barmejo and Angelo Marotte could not be found dead or alive. I have officially listed both men missing and presumed dead.

29 December 1492

The love the savages show their land is touching to see. Their devotion is almost religious. The savages exit the world as they entered it and without any regrets for not having changed or violated it. A good example is the terrace steppes to the west. It is tilled with a symmetry resembling a work of art seen in Rome rather than a field for savages and beasts of burden, the likes of which I've never before seen. When I asked Father Jude how Noah captured and housed all these strange creatures only found in the New World, he just replied, "God works in mysterious ways."

31 December 1492

Over a game of chess tonight, Father Jude told me the Lost Tribe of Israel must be versed in the ways of the Good Book. Father Jude said only the Stairway to Heaven is to be paved in gold, not pagan streets and gutters. Father Jude said the gold in the Eighth City of Cibola would help reunite the Old World with the New. Father Jude said the gold would finance missions, schools, and outposts of Christianity throughout the land. How could I say no? I know with leadership comes tough decisions. I just wish there were an easier way. If I didn't endear myself to the Zuni savages, it wouldn't be a difficult decision.

1 January 1493

The New Year begins with the evacuation and destruction of the City of Gold. The process of melting, recasting, and storing the gold in order to ship it back to Spain is a never-ending process that the men have undertaken with little or no complaints. Father Jude told me God delivered us to these savage shores to rescue his lost children and return them to the fold. The savages are reluctant participants and weep and fall at my feet begging me to leave their homes alone. How can I change my duties and loyalties to God, King, and Country? It is hard for me to look at their savage faces, which days earlier smiled in my presence. I only wanted to raze a few buildings, but Father Jude told me the entire city must come down to finance the worldwide fight against Satan for generations to come.

20 January 1493

What has gotten into me? I'm controlled now by some unseen force. I'm not alone in this hostile takeover. We are all out of character. It's more than gold fever. It's another kind of sickness, only one that has no jungle cure. What it is, I do not know. All I know is I never had anyone tortured, beaten, whipped or garroted. Now it's an everyday occurrence. For King and Country you can justify any barbaric act. I am living proof. All I ever wanted was to be like Prince Henry the Navigator. Now I am everything and everything else. How can this possibly be God's will?

1 February 1493

Today we converted 11,475 buildings into 8450 ton ingot, 6320 ton plate, and 5275 bar. We work nonstop day and night; none of us can really sleep. The savages cry as frightened children in the dark. It's enough to wake the dead. Hearing a million voices howling at once is most unsettling. Father Jude has assured me this is all for their own savage good.

1 February 1493

Melt, form, cast, haul, store that is our daily drudgery. The men are now working twice as hard due to a devastating plague that has swept through the valley. With biblical smite, it has struck down the savages. Initial estimates put the death toll at nearly 300,000 savages. The savages believe Jesus is punishing them. Father Jude has been instrumental in spreading this charge. All remaining healthy savages now willingly comply with my orders. There is no longer a need for whippings to set a good example. Many savages even assist us in reducing their homes to bars of gold. Father Jude says we are only recasting dreams. He insists, "It's the Lord's way."

14 April 1493

Easter Sunday and Christ's resurrection coincides with the last freestanding building being melted in the Eighth City of Cibola. Father Jude proclaims it an auspicious omen that the rising of The One should correspond with the death of the many. Today at morning mass, the savages were present in European dress. Father Jude's message of nakedness being a sin has been well received by the savages. Father Jude says we took away their pagan temples and gave them the Kingdom of God. I still can't believe 5,000 years has been reduced to this. It saddens me, not only for the homes forever lost, but the beauty that was once part of this lush and peaceful valley.

27 April 1493

The Santa Maria and Nina are loaded well beyond capacity. The gold we are taking back to Spain is a mere pittance to the stores I leave behind. The Eighth City of Cibola no longer exists. It's as if it too just disappeared like Marotte and Barmejo. With limited room aboard His Majesty's ships, I'll have to leave more men with those I have already assigned to guard our gold from thieves and brigands. Skeleton crews will have to be supplemented by savages. Being smaller and lighter, they will require less rations and stores aboard our ships. Father Jude volunteered to remain with his New World flock as he now calls the baptized savages. Heawock will accompany me aboard the Santa Maria as interpreter and liaison to the ship's savages. Since I taught Heawock how to play chess, he has become an able student of the game. Still, the young savage doesn't know when to sacrifice a pawn to obtain a greater hold of the board. He fails to grasp the underlying concept that you can be stronger with one less man standing at your side. Martin Pinzon will also remain behind at the colony as second in command to my brother Diego. In a few days we will embark for Spain with riches unknown and unseen by any King and Queen in the civilized world. How our mission has changed since our departure from Spain nine months ago. Father Jude says it was Divine Providence to not only have found the Lost Tribe of Israel, but to have discovered gold in the New World.

5 May 1493

Six days out at sea and we still have favorable trade winds. I could not have asked for more ideal conditions. Since the death of Angelo Marotte, I have taken command of the bridge as navigator aboard the Santa Maria. We are on parallel with Cape St. Vincent. At present speed, we should reach port in six weeks! Godspeed!

28 May 1493

It's been over a week now without a breath of air or ripple of white cap. The sea, as the air, is still and lifeless. I have never seen the Atlantic so flat and becalmed. We chart our daily progress in feet rather than leagues.

1 June 1493

Still nothing moves! We are helpless. The men are weary and restless from inactivity and boredom. Our waste stays where we dispose it off the stern of the ship. The stench is intolerable at times. The cramped quarters only aggravates the men's circumstances. Hostilities between the crew and savages is no longer masked or taken below deck. I know I can't have fighting in the ranks with this most precious cargo on board. I must do something soon, if only to show the men I am still in command.

8 June 1943

A steady westerly wind blossoms the canvas. Such a beautiful sight! Still, we are not moving fast enough. Water and other rations are running dangerously low. As we approach the Old World, we run the risk of encountering that dread of the high seas, corsairs[60]*. Tonight, after dinner, I ordered six savages overboard.*

15 June 1493

Heawock asked me what kind of Sky Father is this Jesus who likes to sacrifice his children? "Why throw good life away when you can cast dead metal into salty waters?" I told the young savage that life is a lot cheaper. The savage fails to understand God's will. Father Jude says it will take time for the savages to become good Christians. Lost children are to be slowly introduced into the light as to not scare them away. Tonight, after dinner, I ordered three more savages overboard.

27 June 1493

I assured Heawock I would not cast him into the sea like Jonah. The young savage asked why the Holy Bible is called the Good Book when it is so full of war and killing and ugly things. I told the young savage it is a never-ending battle to preserve the word of God. He asked, "Is that why oral guardians in the Eighth City of Cibola were burned at the stake?" I tried to connect his question to God's mysterious ways. I told him the oral guardians didn't want to hear the truth in the Good Book. "So sick must find cure with big medicine man in Sky Court," Heawock concluded in his young savage way. Sometimes our oral exchanges are as revealing to me as they are to him. The young savage still looks confused while citing scripture or talking about Jesus.

Occasionally, he lapses back into his old savage ways by discarding his Christian garb for barefoot and naked ass. I grant him these reversals because he is young and far away from the only world he has ever known. It is only temporary and always in the privacy of my quarters. Heawock doesn't understand why his body has to be covered up because of Adam and Eve's boo-boo. Tonight, after dinner, I ordered five more savages overboard.

1 July 1493

Just before supper, Sanchez, sailor on the second watch, informed me that Heawock jumped ship. Sanchez said the young savage ripped off his Sunday clothes, laughed hysterically, and then flung himself over the top rail never to surface again. The poor savage! He was so confused. Lately, he even refused to play chess, saying games of killing haunted his deeper sleep. It sounds as if Heawock went loco. It's been known to happen on long voyages. I pray the good Lord will have mercy on his savage soul.

17 July 1493

When I entered the court at Palos today, King Ferdinand and Queen Isabella offered me, Cristobal Colon, a stool. In all my life, I have never been so honored. As my reward, the "Castle and Lion" will be upon my family crest with a hereditary clause that my descendants will be nobles until the Earth revolves no more. With the gold I have secured from the New World, King Ferdinand and Queen Isabella are now the richest royal couple in the world. I told his Majesty that I would require fleets of galleons to retrieve the remaining stores of gold in the New World Colony. Queen Isabella told me everything would soon be made ready for me to set sail as Admiral of the New World Fleet and Governor of New Spain.

I read on until I came upon 25 September 1493. That was the day Columbus embarked Cadiz with a flotilla of seventeen galleons headed for the New World. The next hundred or so pages detailed rape, torture, slavery, war, and genocide, the likes of which the World had never seen before. I then flipped over scores of more pages until I happened upon this ominous passage.

19 February 1506

What have I wrought? What have I done? To the New World, I imported all the Old World sickness and vices. The Zuni and Arrowacki are extinct. In fourteen years, millions of innocent savages have been killed because of me and my dream. How was I supposed to know I had the Devil aboard the Santa Maria? All the time, I thought I was a knight in God's command, when all along I was a pawn in Satan's hands. Just as my namesake, I too was betrayed and imprisoned. But my sentence has been temporarily commuted. I know I can't run and hide forever. Eventually, the navigator will discover me too. The Cartusian monks have granted me asylum at their mountain monastery outside Paris. I can no longer return to Spain or any of her New World Colonies. I have been condemned and hunted for practicing Judaism by Torquemada's Inquisition. My Book of Prophecies was written to help liberate Jerusalem and make things right in the eyes of our Lord and Savior, Jesus Christ. Day and night I remain a prisoner, locked away in my allotted room where there are no windows or fireplace. One does not know how far the Evil Eye can see. Father Bruno, head of the Sacred Order here, informed me the early Vatican Astrologers knew the Earth was round. The Flat Earth theory was given Papal Decree because the Church Fathers wanted to contain and isolate Satan in the Old World. They didn't want to battle the Forces of Evil on two fronts. Now it makes sense why Pope Alexander was willing to put me under house arrest; it was only to keep Satan from escaping to poison another paradise with his Apple Trick. What a fool I've been. I was so willing a participant in my own self-deceit. Father Bruno cautioned me even in this safe house of Jesus to never invite anyone into my room. He said the Prince of Darkness cannot enter a doorway unless he is invited and asked to have a seat, or in my particular case, a berth on the Santa Maria. Damn Cardinal DeMore, that pimp of Lucifer!

The journal's last entry was dated: *2 May 1506*

The following morning, Columbus was found burned to death in his bed at the monastery. How his journal got from that monastery in Paris to New York is still a mystery and will forever remain one. Tucked away between the last page and back cover was another loose leaf. At first I thought it was another journal entry that had come loose from the spine. But as I picked it up I saw it was another contract, only this one was signed in the blood of King Ferdinand and daughter of Baal[61], Queen Isabella of Spain, the first and second parties to this murder and rape in progress in the New World.

Chapter Eleven

What words can do justice to what I felt at that moment? To know Mr. Leach was not only the BIG BRIT and TALL SPANIARD, but the Devil himself. I knew I had to take the journal. My only regret was not having time to go through those other filing cabinets on Washington, Napoleon, Stalin, and Shakespeare. God can only imagine the deals those men cut. Not only was I running out of time, I was also fearful for my life. I mean, how often does one rifle through the Devil's most prized possessions? I might not have found what I was looking for, but I found something far greater. I didn't solve just three murders, but millions!

Maybe it was fear or paranoia, or maybe a little of both, but I couldn't get over the feeling that I was being watched. By who or what I didn't want to know. If I was quiet and unassuming before, I was even more so now. I made church mice sound as revelers of Bacchus[62].

With the journal wrapped in one hand and my insulated flashlight in the other, I began to work my way towards the procession of granite stairs. My head was on a swivel, forever looking forward, forever looking back. I couldn't stop wondering if I had gone beyond curiosity's threshold. Did I have enough petard[63] to hoist me to the surface without blowing up in my face first? As you know, sometimes Square One is the hardest to get back to. There was at least one consolation—I couldn't blame ignorance for my dilemma. After all, I had to know beyond the shadow of a doubt if that fire was stolen from Heaven or borrowed from Hell.

But would this knowledge prove to be my undoing? Experience only means you have a bigger asshole. Sure, there was still much to see and do down here, but there was always the consolation of tomorrow. Besides, I would be better prepared for the travails along the Match Head Way. More importantly, I would have water. Sweet, sweet water! And despite it being the same sweaty nightmare, it would be a different day. I know it sounds absurd, but it's no more absurd than being fundamentally sound and tone deaf.

Even before I began my ascent, I could hear vindictive rumblings bubbling down below. The vertical vents running alongside the stairwell discharged more than blasts of stifling heat, but enraged, wrathful shrieks. Down Stygian shafts I could now see fireballs percolating and assuming a kind of subhuman form. It was as if the furies were being released from the dungeons of hell. I don't know how else to rationalize it, but the fire was somehow embodied as it scaled those netherworld chimneys in pursuit of me.

I had never run so fast in all my life. Then again, I never had any reason to. I was always the one doing the tracking and running down. It was different now, for I was the thief being chased by the heat.

There was no let up, no pausing to catch my breath, not even when I went through the great crypt to pick up that other stairwell. I was running for my life and there is nothing figurative whatsoever about that statement. I ran like hell—in hell. How many people can actually claim that on their 10K resume? Where I had the stamina and strength to accomplish this extraordinary feat I still don't know. A jolt of adrenaline only lasts a few minutes at most. But this rush, this outburst of energy, fueled me throughout my climb to the surface. Survival, being an instinctive mechanism, can no more be taught than drummed out of our inner core. All my energy was dedicated to living to see another day, if only to set the record straight.

Getting out in one piece was no longer a consideration. Just getting out alive with the journal was all that mattered to me. Such things sound so melodramatic when you're safe and sound and the world makes sense again. When you're out of harm's way, you can afford to be an atheist and immortal fool again. But when you're in a foxhole, it's an entirely different story altogether, and inevitably, it always begins with Genesis.

I never invoked the name of God more than I did on those stairs that day. I've thought since then that maybe that's what got me through this hellish ordeal. I'm not one to believe in miracles or divine intervention. On the other hand, I can't categorically denounce them out right either. Not anymore, never anymore! Those cavalier days are also gone. I've pondered the thought since then, you know, of being pushed up or driven out. To tell you the truth, I really don't know. Maybe I'll have to wait for Judgment Day like everybody else who fosters hope only to adopt wishful thinking.

Onward, upward I fled. There really wasn't much thought involved in the process. All I had to do was place one foot in front of the other. I was more or less on autopilot. I stumbled and lost my balance numerous times during my escape. The uneven stairs seemed to treacherously conspire with my burning eyes. I wish I could get down and dirty and bogged down in salacious details, but I really don't remember much else during that uphill battle. Don't forget, I was in a dark, dingy, smoky stairwell running for my life.—Besides, when instinct kicks in, all else is put on hold. Running to save your skin will narrow every vision and thought to its barest minimum. It's the be-all and end-all of second guesses. Don't get me wrong, I still had my share of fears and panic attacks. How could I ever forget who was chasing me? That I could not avoid, regardless how fast I ran. It was that real, that palpable, even when I stooped to blatant symbolism, of two horns and a pitchfork.

How I was able to see in that Forge of Tophet[64] is another of those ongoing mysteries. Salt and sulfur are a stinging and scalding duo. I also had nothing dry to wipe the sweat forever pouring into my eyes that burned as if they too were on fire. I was running, sweating, and burning, but in varying degrees of nightmarish intensity. But, as I could no more stop, neither could It. One seemingly led right into the other and back again. It was a vicious circle, only one that wouldn't let me go without first extracting a pound of my flagellated flesh.

At what point I lost my flashlight, I don't recall. All I remember was running with the journal tucked under my arm like a gridiron pigskin as fiery whiplashes flailed away at my drenched body. Strange as this may sound, it wasn't so much that they were trying to beat me into submission, as they were trying to dislodge and wrestle that journal of Columbus from my hands.

I could feel red hot tongues roaring up and down my spine as Cerberus[65] licked at my burning heels. Talk about hot pursuit! Lash after lash. Step after step. The monotony was as lethal as it was suggestive as it flirtatiously breathed down the nape of my neck.

Sanity may come and go up and down the radio dial, but madness is not so fortunate. For when it arrives, it stays and plays for the remainder of your days.

How many second winds I had, I can't say; all I recall is that final one that pushed me over the top and into the mansion. I furiously raced up the remaining stairs into that extended hallway behind the "Employees Only" door. But I knew I couldn't stop now, not with those vengeful harpies crawling down my back and up my ass. I scurried through meandering corridors until I reached the Main Hall. Suddenly a seismic blast rocked the mansion to its very moorings, knocking me right off my wobbly feet. Remarkably, the mansion was empty, cleaned out with not a stick of furniture surviving the purge. I guess Mr. Leach was serious about going where the Four Rivers of Paradise meet in Szechuan, China.

I was no sooner down than up again and running for dear life. Raging fireballs soon began to consume the mansion, eating it right from underneath me. I just barely made it out the front door when the mansion that had stood for centuries imploded and violently collapsed upon itself like a giant black star taking everything, including light, right down with it. Deliriously, I stumbled out the front door and into the crowded downtown street. I was dehydrated, exhausted, and stripped of every last vestige of dignity and clothing. All that remained were shards and pieces of my gym shoes fused to my raw feet. The journal of Columbus and the contracts were also gone, as if they had never existed in this world or any other. All that survived my underworld odyssey was that pressed leaf that somehow or another ended up balled in my right fist.

That's all I remember before losing consciousness and waking up three days later in the intensive care unit at St. Luke's Hospital. Unlike Shadrach[66], who escaped the fiery furnace unscathed, I sustained third-degree burns over sixty-five percent of my body and face. I lost my right testicle and left pinky. I also lost thirteen pounds. So much for any political aspirations I might have harbored after leaving the police force.

I not only had some catching up to do to bring me up to speed, I had a lot of explaining to do as well—particularly what I was doing naked in the street outside a burning city landmark that hundreds of eyewitnesses saw me run out of moments before it was totally and completely destroyed with great loss of life.

Since Mr. Leach and his employees had been seen entering Lord, Harry, and Gooseberry that fateful morning and hadn't been heard from or seen since, it was assumed they perished in the five alarm blaze. So out of the fire and into the frying pan I went. I was practically on the defensive the moment I awoke. I was now very reluctant to tell what I knew as gospel according to John. I mean, you don't just awake from a coma and accuse a pillar in the world community of being the Devil. How would that play with the brass or the mainstream media? Besides, my physical evidence was gone, along with Mr. Leach. What's more, a half-baked, naked man found laying face down in the gutter does tend to lose all his credibility. Even the Mayor and Chief were reconsidering my elite status as the City's Finest.

How quickly fortunes change. Overnight, I went from a golden boy in first class to a morbid freak in steerage. For several weeks, I even had an armed guard posted outside my hospital room. The general consensus was I snapped from the pressures and strains imposed upon me by the "Crime of the Century." It was very difficult for me to muster any kind of sympathy or support from a cynical, outraged public, especially when it appeared as if City Hall was protecting and covering up for one of its boys in blue. How could I tell my side of the story in this hostile, bellicose environment? I was, after all, the prime suspect in the arson of a historic building. I was also a murder suspect. Editorials pilloried me. Some elected vigilantes espoused the death penalty, "For the great loss to property and life I so wantonly and cravenly caused with malice and reckless disregard." To keep my mouth shut was not only legally imperative, it was also the only way I was going to stay out of Bellevue[67] and of wearing white after Labor Day.

With murder and arson charges hanging over my head as a sword of Damocles[68], I didn't want to make it look like I was trying to cop an insanity plea. Being stuck in this limbo and not knowing which way the evidence would go was painstaking enough. But to have to remain silent with what I knew as the God's honest truth was killing me. As days morphed into weeks, this Crimson Tide was turning more and more against me. From City Hall to the Review Board of Professional Standards, I could count my friends on one finger. No man is stronger than current events regardless how accomplished a swimmer he may be.

The mansion's debris field was so extensive and widespread that it took the better part of two months to comb through, sift and examine. Despite this time-consuming effort, no remains of Mr. Leach or his "familiars" were ever found in the charred rubble. As a matter of fact, not one bone fragment was ever discovered at the site. It was meticulously searched, reminiscent of the Twin Towers in the wake of 9/11. The Fire Marshall, after a six month inquiry, concluded in his official statement released to the press that, "Due to the extraordinary nature of the fire that reached 3000º that the victims were instantly vaporized." He went on to say the blaze was caused by faulty wiring in the old west wing of the historical mansion.

Faulty wiring my ass! That flame not only had a forked tongue, it had a face. Oh yeah, and a name—one that was on the front door of the mansion all along.

CHAPTER TWELVE

With no bodies, and the supposed cause of the blaze determined by the Fire Commission Panel, I was exonerated and cleared of all charges brought against me. However, because of the extent of my injuries, I was forced to retire from the Police Department. At least I had my freedom, or so I thought.

I stayed at St. Luke's for several more weeks recuperating from my wounds, burns, and skin grafts. It wasn't until I was about to check out when a Filipino nurse who was working in the emergency room that fateful day brought me a small plastic bag containing my personal belongings. At first I thought she'd mistaken me for someone else. After all, when I was rushed to the hospital, I was naked as a jaybird. But as I looked at the contents in the bag, I saw the leaf that fell out of Columbus's journal. I had forgotten all about it, which was easy enough to do under the circumstances. The nurse said it must be important because I refused to let go of it when they were trying to run an I.V. in me. I thanked her for her kindness and concern, and then departed St. Luke's with a memento to remind me of a paradise forever lost.

For over a year, I went through a rigorous physical rehabilitation program in order to become mobile and independent again. It, however, was a very slow and arduous process, just as it was to look at myself in the mirror. I no longer could recognize myself. The rugged, handsome face and aquiline nose I had known all my life was gone. I had surgical grafts and plastic surgery performed to restore a semblance of anatomical normalcy to my body and face. However, despite all efforts and attempts, I was still a one-man traveling freak show who always turned heads and instigated youthful snickers.

There was no way back to my past, that too was sealed over, just like that portal to hell below Lord, Harry, and Gooseberry. One cannot forget "what is" to recapture and restore "what was." There was also no more tantalizing lovers or adoring fans to fawn over my every word to justify my existence. I no longer sought half truths while swallowing whole lies. Gradually and painfully, I was coming to terms with this new me who was forged from the fires of hell.

In regards to that leaf, I eventually brought it to Professor Steinmetz at NYU's Department of Botanical Studies to ascertain its provenance[69]. After carbon dating several test samples, I was informed the leaf was from a Middle Eastern species of fig tree called Capricious that had been extinct for over seven thousand years. When Professor Steinmetz inquired as to where I got such a rare and unusual find, I simply told him, "I found it in an old book from an old friend."

I keep mostly to myself nowadays. Every so often I scan the newspapers for lucky fools who struck it rich or wealthy old goats burned to death beyond recognition. I still can't help but wonder what cycle that Eternal Pyromaniac is on now. How can I not? It's been almost twenty-one years since the three Gombahs were smoked like cheap cigars in their penthouse. I never invite anyone over, not even for old time's sake. I still recall Father Bruno's advice to Columbus. I no longer cook with gas either. I even had my fireplace bricked up. Now I stick to veggie fare or deli sandwiches at *Manny's*. I also keep away from barbeques. The haunting smell of burning flesh no longer appeals to me and I'm a devout Catholic. Go figure.

GLOSSARY

1. Dervishes—Swirling dancers

2. Svengoulian—Sorcerers

3. Page 6—The gossip page of who's who in New York City

4. Mickey, Yogi, and Whitey—New York Yankee legends: Mickey Mantle, Yogi Berra, Whitey Ford

5. Capistrano—Allusion to swallows

6. Amazin' Mets—New York Mets baseball team who miraculously won the World Series in 1969

7. Fez Heads—Shriners

8. Zoetic—pertaining or relating to life

9. Big Bad Bear—Bear market on Wall Street

10. Bacchanalia—Parties/orgies in Rome

11. Jigs from Kenya—Allusion to Black marathon runners that generally win long races

12. House that Ruth built—Yankee stadium, Babe Ruth

13. Epicurean—One devoted to finer things

14. Casper—The friendly ghost, allusion to the Holy Spirit

15. Crimean—The charge of the Light Brigade in the Crimean

16. Hell Gate—The whirlpools in the narrow channel between Manhattan and Queens in the East river

17. Charybdis—a whirlpool in the Strait of Messina off the NE coast of Sicily

18. Lex Scripta—Written law

19. Babylon—Reference to Daniel and writing on the wall while Jews were in captivity in Babylon

20. Chair—Pope's chair

21. Bellwether's—A ringleader

22. Peter Minuit—Bought Manhattan from natives in 1626

23. Wick theories—A person is burned through his/her own fats after being ignited, accidentally or otherwise

24. Son of Sam—Berkowitz, killer in New York City circa 1980

25. Ad Quem—End point

26. Sevens preceding the sixes—Craziness

27. Wasp Nests—White Anglo Saxon Protestants

28. Astor's Ballroom—The number of people that could be counted as members of the Fashionable Society could fit into the Astor's ballroom

29. Cook's tour—Quick, cheap tour

30. Cubit—ancient measure

31. Wyverns—Dragons

32. Syllogism—Two premises and a conclusion

33. Pig theory—Slang for cops

34. Six cylinders—Six senses

35. Bohemian Club—Private retreat noted for its bizarre rituals and practices

36. Belmont—Famous racetrack in New York

37. Blue Book—Book used for police codes and conduct

38. Kitty Genovese—Woman stabbed to death in Queens in front of many witnesses that did nothing

39. B and E—Breaking and entering

40. Bon mot—A witty remark or comment

41. Gibbous—Phase of the moon when it is more than half, but not totally full

42. Argus—Monster with many eyes

43. Auscultated—Listening to internal sounds

44. Myopia—Near-sightedness

45. Eurydice—After she was taken to Hades Orpheus went to retrieve her

46. Rent—Hole, gash

47. Miasma—Fog, haze

48. Five Points—Area in NYC reputed for gangs

49. City of Gehenna—Where the ancient king Ahaz and Manasseh were said to have sacrificed their sons to Moloch, the Devil, the evil one

50. Soniferous—Sound echoes

51. Mint of Juno—Regal Queen of the gods

52. Mine of Goloconda—Rich mine

53. Amaranth—Imaginary flower that never dies or fades

54. Frontispiece—an illustrated leave preceding the title page of a book

55. Gonfalon—Long flag or banner

56. Pillars of Hercules—Rock of Gibraltar

57. Cathay—Ancient name of China

58. Astrolabe—Instrument used before the sextant to find the altitude of a star

59. Salic—Harsh laws

60. Corsairs—Pirates

61. Baal—A God, meaning "master" or "lord"

62. Bacchus—God of wine and revelry

63. Petard—Explosives

64. Forge of Tophet—Location in Jerusalem where children were sacrificed to the gods

65. Cerberus—Three headed hound that guarded the gates of hell

66. Shadrach—One of three captives in Babylon who came out of the fiery furnace miraculously unharmed

67. Bellevue—Mental institution

68. Sword of Damocles—Any situation threatening imminent harm or disaster.

69. Provenance—Place or source of origin